Sent to the River God Forgot is a readable story of ⟨...⟩
and me learn that we need never fear that God ⟨...⟩
authors, discover that all of us at some time ar⟨...⟩
choices no one should have to make. God has w⟨...⟩
American Evangelical textbook to achieve his best for us and for
others through us.

Profit, as I did, from this account of an overseas encounter. It will
help you "Stay on the path; keep the Chief in sight; continue to follow even when your knees ache or your heart breaks." Ultimately
such commitment to Christ leads to contentment and victory.

    —*Curtis B. Akenson, Ph.D.*
      Pastor Emeritus, First Baptist Church of Minneapolis
      Former president, Northwestern College

The Waltons have given us more than a story of opposition, difficulties, and self-denial, all overcome for the sake of the gospel. *Sent to the
River God Forgot* places the tragedy of a forgotten people in its proper
historical context, giving a depth that many stirring missionary
accounts omit. The Muinanes people were not really forgotten, just
forgotten by the church. Rubber robbers (euphemistically called rubber barons) used them, slaughtered them, and stole their rubber
resources. Only when the rubber market was gone did the "barons"
forget them.

When the world again "remembered" the Muinanes, it was for the
cocaine that their homelands could produce. Again, death and
destruction. But between the rubber and the cocaine, the gospel of
Jesus did come; God had not forgotten.

In *Sent to the River God Forgot* there is deeper insight than in familiar
"missionary stories." More than accounts of snakes and spiders, disease and demons, and heroic self-denial, it illustrates the essence of
living out the missionary call, "an unending reprocessing of life as we
had known it." Joy and enjoyment are more important in this book
than suffering and sorrow.

Read this book for more than an adventure story. Read it to learn
how God works in mind, heart, and spirit to bring men to himself.

    —*Donald K. Smith, Ph.D.*
      Chair, Division of Intercultural Studies
      Western Seminary

The Waltons have written a touching story of discovery among the
Muinanes tribe in the jungle regions of Colombia. In this adventure
of faithfulness and perseverance, we experience the heartwarming
best of an encounter between two North American missionaries and
the Muinanes as the gospel transforms them both. They tell of two
little girls, both of whom should have died and did not, and, through
this act of God's grace, the gospel comes to the kind of people the

world often forgets. Open to learning from each other, the gospel gently placed in context, this story illustrates much of what contemporary missiology says is important to modern mission.

—*Bryant L. Myers,*
Vice President for Mission and Evangelism
World Vision International

How well I remember when Jim, Jan, and their two little ones, Diana and Danny, arrived at Lomalinda, Wycliffe's Center in Colombia. Having just finished reading the exciting manuscript, I praise God for their faith, courage, and victory in giving the Muinanes the New Testament in their own language.

It isn't easy to share one's disappointments as well as victories, but Jim and Jan did just that. During those early years, when some of their work was done at Lomalinda, my mother was with us and started a preschool for the children of the translators. Danny was one of those three year olds who won his way into Mother's heart. It's easy to see how Diana and Danny played a big part in making friendships. May the happy memories of these two children growing up in the jungle without any conveniences, and yet counting those years as the highlight of their lives, be an encouragement to other young couples taking their little ones to other people groups whose languages have never yet been written. Thanks to you, Jim and Jan!

—*Elaine (Mrs. Cameron) Townsend,*
Wycliffe Bible Translators

This book was good reading as well as thought provoking. The book has it all—the joys as well as the realities of trials experienced in bringing God's Word to people living in a tropical jungle. I was repeatedly reminded of our own translation program among the Samo in another jungle half a world away on the island of New Guinea. Missiologically the book contains many insights—cultural relevance, the place of Scripture in the growth of Christian faith, church growth principles of discipling and perfecting. The reality of the narrative and the strength of character—both the Waltons and the Muinanes—make this a valuable contribution to our understanding of how God uses his Word and his people to conform all who trust him to his image. God has a wonderful plan, reaching people who feel as though God forgot them and encouraging their response when they discover that he already knows them intimately, and communicates it through the Word—both in flesh (as the Waltons lived among the Muinanes) and in print (as the message became available to them).

—*R. Daniel Shaw*
Director, Bible Translation Program,
Fuller Theological Seminary

SENT TO THE RIVER
GOD FORGOT

SENT TO *The River God Forgot*

JIM AND JANICE WALTON

Tyndale House Publishers, Inc.
WHEATON, ILLINOIS

Editing and additional rewriting by Cindy L. Maddox, SilverFire Editorial Services

Unless otherwise indicated, Scripture quotations are taken from the *Holy Bible,* King James Version.

Scripture verses marked TLB are taken from *The Living Bible,* copyright © 1971 owned by assignment by KNT Charitable Trust. All rights reserved.

Scripture quotations marked NIV are taken from the *Holy Bible,* New International Version®. Copyright © 1973, 1978, 1984 by International Bible Society. Used by permission of Zondervan Publishing House. All rights reserved. The "NIV" and "New International Version" trademarks are registered in the United States Patent and Trademark Office by International Bible Society. Use of either trademark requires permission of International Bible Society.

Library of Congress Cataloging-in-Publication Data

Walton, James W., date
     Sent to the river God forgot / Jim and Janice Walton.
        p.   cm.
     ISBN 0-8423-5977-X
     1. Muinane Indians—Missions.   2. Walton, James W., 1938-
3. Walton, Janice.   4. Indians of South America—Missions—Columbia.
I. Walton, Janice.   II. Title.
F2270.2.M75W35   1995
266′.0089′98—dc20   95-6408

Printed in the United States of America

00 99 98 97 96 95
 8   7   6   5   4   2   1

This book is lovingly dedicated to
DIANA and DANIEL
who, as children, and now as adults,
share our vision for missions,
participate in the work,
inspire and encourage us,
love and respect all cultures and people.
They are true examples of all the wonderful MKs
(missionary kids)
who bless their parents and
make them better missionaries.

A birthday present.
from Brian & Marion.
July 1995.

CONTENTS

In 1968, Richard Collier wrote a book entitled *The River That God Forgot* (New York: E. P. Dutton & Co., 1968). He told terrible stories of the Amazon rubber boom and the atrocities inflicted upon the inhabitants of the Amazon jungles in the world's quest for raincoats, tires, and rubber balls. When God called us to this part of the world—to the small village of La Sabana, deep in the heart of the Colombian jungle—we wondered if we were moving our family to a forgotten, God-forsaken land. But on those jungle trails we found the footprints of God, who had gone before us and who walked with us every step of the way.

Over the past twenty-five years, many have suggested that we write the amazing story of our experiences with the Muinanes and "The River That God Forgot." We were reluctant to do so for three reasons. First, we were too busy living it to write about it. Second, we had never written a book, and we didn't know how to begin. And third, we were uncertain how today's modern reader would relate to our experiences among an unreached people in the middle of a tropical jungle; or for that matter, the potential missionary who in today's world will likely serve in very different circumstances.

God took care of the first reason through time. After leaving Colombia, we joined the international administration of the Summer Institute of Linguistics (SIL), the organization with which we served in Columbia. Since our energy was no longer divided between flying in and out of the jungle, cooking on a mud stove, and translating day and night, we now had the weekends and evenings to write these stories of God's marvelous grace.

God took care of the second problem through our friend and author Harry Farra. When Harry and his wife, Vonnie, came to visit us in Dallas, we told them about the numerous requests we had received to write this book. The Farras encouraged us further, and Harry offered his help with the manuscript. During the writing of this book, Harry played a unique role as adviser and mentor. He guided us through the many minefields and pitfalls of our manuscript and contributed a solid awareness that "a well-told story teaches its own lesson." Our gratitude goes out to this dear friend for his numerous insights about writing, as well as his endless encouragement.

The third reason for our uncertainty took a bit more work on God's part. The more we became acquainted with today's mission challenges, which lie largely with the "partially reached" and the "resistant" people groups, and the longer we lived back in the States, the more we realized that the problems and struggles Americans face are not unlike those we faced in the jungle. The scenery in our town may be different, but personal struggles are similar. Whether we drive on a concrete highway or walk along a jungle trail, difficulties, temptations, and trials await us. God's message and God's help are just as real and just as needed in the world's cities as they are in the jungles of Amazonia. These are not simply the stories of a missionary family in Colombia. They are stories of conquering fear, overcoming obstacles, learning much-needed lessons, trusting the Lord, and discovering God's presence in our lives. Sound familiar? They are probably much like the stories of your own life.

We want to offer a few words of explanation before you begin. Today, terms quickly rise to favor and just as quickly fall into disfavor. Were we in the *jungle* or in the *tropical rain forest?* Was Manuel a *shaman* or a *medicine man?* Some anthropologists and students of anthropology might object to our using the word *tribe* to refer to the people with whom we lived, for they consider this a pejorative label, signaling attitudes of superiority. Others might object to our using the common term *Indians* rather than the more accurate but cumbersome term *indigenous people groups.*

Terminology in relation to ethnic minorities and the world's people groups is changing. Historically the word *tribe* was both acceptable and correct. In many areas of the world, and among many of the world's people, the term continues to be held in high regard. Our use of the term, however, is more a convenience than a stance. During the time we lived and worked with the Muinanes in Colombia, *tribe* was—and seems to remain—the most acceptable term to identify the many people groups living in the nation's jungle areas. We desire that our attitude toward the Muinanes be found in our hearts and not in the uncertain connotations of vocabulary.

We also want to offer our thanks where it is due:

To Mom Walton for her help in editing the manuscript.

To all our SIL colleagues and friends in Colombia and around the world. It is our high privilege to serve with such a faithful family. Thanks be to God for what he is doing!

To the Muinanes, to whom we are deeply indebted for allowing us to live many of the most important years of our lives in La Sabana. They invited us into their community, their families, and their hearts. We came to love and respect them, and we shared with them the little we had — our lives and our faith.

To Cindy Maddox, SilverFire Editorial Services, who brought her knowledge of good storytelling to the manuscript.

To Wendell Hawley, Dan Elliott, Wightman Weese, and all those of Tyndale House Publishers who gave of their abilities to make this book what it ought to be.

To our many friends, family, teachers, pastors, counselors, mentors, and prayer partners. And to countless others we don't even know: those who gave money to support our efforts, provided us a place to stay when we traveled, listened to our stories, and shared our trials and our triumphs. God has brought so many wonderful people into our lives. We are thoroughly humbled by your lives and your friendship. Next to God, we are most blessed by — and most indebted to — you, our friends.

Thank you for reading this book and spending your time to discover that God never forgot the river, or the people along the river. May you also discover the God who loves you. As you read the pages of this book and become acquainted with the Muinanes and the marvelous workings of a wonderful God, may you experience his personal touch in your life. We are totally convinced that God is able to meet any and every need of your life.

Jim and Janice Walton
Dallas, Texas

CHAPTER ONE

Does This Jungle Have a Map?

He is the Way
Follow Him through the Land of Unlikeness
And you will see rare beasts,
And have unique Adventures.
        —W. H. Auden in "Christmas Oratorio"

JIM'S STORY

"You're moving *where?* But *why?*"

"You'll be so far from home."

"You have plenty of ministry opportunities right where you are."

"Do you really want to raise your children in a *jungle?*"

When we told our friends and family that we were planning to go to Colombia, they thought we had lost our minds. And in the eyes of the world, we probably *were* crazy. We were abandoning our culture, leaving behind the relatively high standard of living we enjoyed in the United States, and moving far away from our loved ones. But the insistent word of God's calling silenced all other voices. Yes, we would be living under primitive conditions and ministering unnoticed. True, we would be far from our loved ones and would miss them terribly between visits. Undoubtedly, our children would encounter challenges that their counterparts in the States would not experience. But our faith was simple: When God called, we answered. Our answer was yes.

As most people in our situation would do, we continually searched for signs of certainty before making such a drastic move. We had full assurance from the Scriptures and from the way all the events of our decision fell into place that we were in the center of God's plan. Still, we had doubts and fears of the unknown. Did God know where Colombia was, and did he have a map through the jungle?

The decision was not made lightly or quickly; once we had set our hearts and minds toward our new adventure, however, we were eager to begin. Unfortunately, one of the first lessons missionaries must learn is patience. To me it seemed that our journey to Colombia was taking forever.

We left Minnesota's subzero temperatures on the day after Christmas, 1963. The long journey took us through Miami, Panama, and finally to Bogotá. Throughout the trip, we somehow managed to carry the necessary carry-on baggage and still hold tightly to two-year-old Danny and three-year-old Diana. We lost neither luggage nor children, which is nearly a miracle in itself!

Soon after we settled into the Summer Institute of Linguistics' (SIL) guest house in Bogotá, we began Spanish study at the University of the Andes. I grew up in Minnesota and Jan in Wisconsin, and neither of us had studied

Spanish. We quickly came to love this beautiful language. The purity of the vowel sounds, the complexity of the verbs, and the vibrant trill of the *rr* rolled easily from native speakers' tongues—and later from the tongues of our own children, who seemed unimpeded by past language habits.

Jan and I struggled to learn as much Spanish as possible in the short three-month course. In truth, I struggled more than Jan. Both of us, however, longed to get to our real task: to be out in a village somewhere, learning one of the unwritten languages.

First, we had to select the village, a group with whom we could live to observe their culture, study their language, and ultimately translate the Scriptures. SIL's director, Clarence Church, assured us that the mission administration would work with us, guiding us in our choice, but the ultimate decision was ours.

Approximately seventy-eight languages are spoken in Colombia, with language groups ranging in size from 100 members to as many as 100,000. Our administrators directed our attention to one of the languages of southeastern Colombia in the state of Vaupés, where some twelve to fifteen language groups needed translations. This area, with its concentration of language groups, offered an ideal situation for a young mission with limited resources to reach the greatest number of people in the shortest time. If most missionary-linguist teams were allocated close together, it would be easier to care for each other and provide logistical support such as air transportation, radio communication, local government, and church relations. Non-Catholic educators, missionaries, and others had not been welcome in many areas of the country for years. With a window of opportunity open to the Vaupés, the administration wanted to allocate as many teams as possible, not knowing if or when that window might close again.

We listened, and we prayed; but we had no peace regarding any of the language groups of the Vaupés. We wondered what God knew that we didn't know. We felt that we must find out God's plan for us. If not the Vaupés, where? And why? The answer to the first question was not long in coming. The second question was not answered for many years.

The "where" was Colombia's southernmost state of Amazonas, which was also in the jungle, and not open to foreigners. As members of SIL, we were allowed into these areas only because we had a contract with the Colombian government to study the phonetics and morphology of Colombia's languages and provide information and translation services to the government.

The people that God led us to were the Muinane (*Mwee·náh·nay*); the village was La Sabana. La Sabana lay half a degree below the equator, deep in the jungle and precisely in that area Richard Collier wrote about in his book, *The River That God Forgot* (New York: E. P. Dutton & Co., 1968). Though the Muinanes lived beyond the reach of most civilization, they had been touched cruelly by the horrors of the *casa Arana*—the household of a Peruvian rubber baron, Julio Arana, who exploited the jungles and their inhabitants in search of rubber.

The Muinanes had suffered torture, slavery, death, and near genocide at the hands of white "rubber hunters."

They called the outsiders "gun people/shooting people." All who came from the outside brought guns and death. Could we expect the Muinanes to welcome us, or even allow us to stay? How could we dare dream that we might be allowed to live on their land, learn their language, walk their trails, travel their rivers, and touch their children?

We received no handwriting on the wall, felt no earthquake, saw no fire—just a sure, small voice within us that led us to the Muinanes. Was this an impossible dream? Yes. But nevertheless we felt a strange peace and confidence that God could somehow transform the dream into reality. We went with the full blessing of our mission administrators.

On July 3, 1964, Jan, Diana, and Dan waved goodbye as fellow linguist Stan Schauer and I left Lomalinda, SIL's newly established mission center 175 miles southeast of Bogotá. Jan and the children would set up housekeeping in a one-room cabin at the center while I went to find the Muinanes and our new home.

At the border town of Pto Leguízamo, we met up with JAARS pilot Forrey Zander. (JAARS—Jungle Aviation and Radio Service—is the technical service and support division of SIL.) Forrey and his Aeronca seaplane would fly us into the Amazon jungle, but we would still have a two-day walk to La Sabana.

Early the next morning, Stan and Forrey and I made our way to the river. The little Aeronca, bobbing up and down on its floats, waited to carry us into the Amazon. After loading our supplies, the engine revved and we were off—or should have been. The floats rode deep in the water. We roared down the river. We roared up the river. We turned around again and again, trying to take off. If I remember correctly, Forrey only grunted when I jokingly suggested we taxi the whole way to La Sabana.

"The floats must have taken on water," Forrey informed us. "Now that we've burned off some fuel and some weight, there's no other reason for the problem."

We taxied to the river's edge, climbed out onto the pontoons, removed the covers, and dipped a sponge into the pontoon. We squeezed the water from the sponge back into the river, until our hands were like ice and the floats were dry inside. Still we were unable to take off. We had to eliminate some cargo.

Over the next few years, it seemed that every time we flew in or out of La Sabana, we argued with ourselves over what could be left behind. Even today, after a twenty-year-long object lesson, I find myself tempted to add too much baggage to my life.

Once in the air, my mind settled back to thinking about what might be ahead of us. The plane's single engine droned slowly on above the Putumayo River as we headed for the little town of El Encanto. We would land there on the wide placid river to refuel.

"Don't waste time at El Encanto," Stan and I had been warned. "The blood-sucking gnats are a plague and will eat you alive." The warning was accurate. The gnats swarmed in huge swirling clouds around our face and neck, arms and hands. The next day we looked as if we had the measles; our bodies were covered with little red spots the size of pinheads. We later learned that the gnats were everywhere. At some places and at certain times during the year, they were worse — but always the gnats, the incessant gnats!

We wrestled a fifty-five-gallon drum of fuel, stored ahead of time in the only house at El Encanto, down the riverbank. With a short length of plastic hose, we siphoned the aviation fuel into a five-gallon bucket, which was handed up to the pilot, who in turn poured the fuel into the wing tanks of the plane. We passed bucket after bucket until the tanks were full or the drum was empty, and we gained new appreciation for self-serve gas pumps.

Back in the air, we were on the final leg of our flight into the jungle. We circled the Catholic mission and boarding school at La Chorrera before landing on the river. Although half a dozen Muinane children were at the school, we would not meet them. To reach La Sabana, we would somehow have to arrange for someone to guide us over the trail.

No one expected us. No one knew we were coming. They had no phones, no mail service, no means of communication with the outside world. As soon as we arrived, people began to emerge from the mission, the school, the houses, the fields, and the jungle. It was not a large group of people, but everyone came, as visitors are unusual in the jungle. We tried to greet everyone in Spanish. A few seemed to understand. Then we made our way up the hill to greet and formally introduce ourselves to the mission staff.

The priest and nuns graciously received, fed, and cared for us. We were told that the few Muinane children at the school had arrived only a day or two before, along with

Fernando, chief of the Muinanes. We could hardly believe our ears. Could it be that the very chief of the Muinanes might take us to La Sabana? Some might call it a coincidence, but I called it a miracle.

The next morning Stan and I began our journey by trail to La Sabana, with the Muinane chief leading us. I had imagined the jungle as flat, but I discovered a series of streams and hills. The lush green carpet I expected was mostly dirt with a mat of rotting leaves, twigs, and branches. These form an important part in the almost closed growth cycle of the jungle. Nutrients that fall to the ground rapidly decay in the heat and abundant rains, and they are quickly absorbed by the huge, shallow roots of the jungle trees. Few nutrients penetrate deep into the soil. If the jungle is cleared, the nutrients are soon leached from the soil by exposure to sun and rain.

We walked under a huge canopy of trees, towering eighty to one hundred feet overhead. Beneath the canopy were other trees, plants, bushes, flowers (though mostly hidden and hard to see at first), insects, animals, and birds. The hilly jungle floor was carved up by dozens of streams that crisscrossed and wound back and forth across the path. We sloshed through the shallow streams, inched our way across slippery logs over larger streams, and climbed and descended more hills than I can count. At one of the many places where the trail plunged down-hill, Stan reached out to grab onto something to slow his descent. The tree trunk was covered with four-inch thorns. The tips broke off easily and left themselves buried in his hand.

About four-thirty in the afternoon, we stopped at a large

thatch dwelling, the home of a family of Huitoto Indians. It was the only house on the trail, and these were the only people we had seen all day. We had heard that vast areas of the jungle were still uninhabited. I was beginning to realize just how isolated my little family would be.

Stan and I went to bed early that night rather than lingering long before the fire. We slept in cloth hammocks strung between poles. It felt good to retire from the strange sounds of languages not yet understood. From my hammock I stared up at the smoke-blackened leaf roof that formed a thirty-foot-high ceiling between us and the stars. I rubbed the back of my legs behind my knees. The aches and pains seemed to bring a sense of reality to the day. So much of what was happening felt like a dream.

For more than ten years, since I was twelve, I had dreamed of being a missionary. I heard no voices, saw no visions; but God did speak to me in the stillness of my heart and through his Word. My parents never preached, nor persuaded, nor, as far as I recall, even suggested what we three boys should do with our lives. Instead, they modeled a Christian life and said to each of us, "God will lead you in the best plan for you. We trust you to find that plan, and, wherever it takes you, you have our blessing." God's plan led my oldest brother to the pastorate, my middle brother into industry, and me to the mission field.

Lying in my hammock in the jungle, so far away from anything I had ever known, I began to flip through some of the favorite memories in my mind—such as Sunday dinners at my parents' house when I was in high school and college.

We were in the habit of bringing friends home for Sunday dinner, and Mama Walton never knew if she would be feeding five or fifteen until we got home from church and sat down at the table. Although our family lived on a modest income, and we were told that there was not enough money for many things, my dad never once hinted that our Sunday dinner was the largest part of the weekly food bill. My mom never worried—to our knowledge—if there would be enough food. There always was.

What were we thinking? Did we believe that God would stretch the kettle of potatoes and the little roast, as he did the widow of Zarephath's cruse of oil and tiny amount of meal? Likely, we boys never thought about it at the time. But lying in the jungle, I thought about it then.

Mom, Dad, I'm here. I'm not at the Muinane village yet, but I'll be there tomorrow. God brought me here, just like you knew he would. I'm a little apprehensive. There are lots of unknowns ahead, but I'm happy and so excited. I can't wait to get a house started and go back and get Jan and Diana and Danny. It's finally happening. We are missionaries!

Was there a little pride in that last part? Sure, maybe so. Eventually I would learn that location doesn't make a missionary, and everyone is called to go to their neighbors and bring them the Good News of Christ's love. I would also learn that being a foreign missionary wasn't all glamor, joy, and excitement. But I was thankful and pleased. God would deal with my pride later.

Before daylight the next morning, we started walking. The chief knew how far we had to travel before darkness fell on the jungle and how fast we had walked the previous day. It was even harder keeping up the second day, but we dared not lose sight of our guide. He could descend a hill to a stream, cross the log, and climb the other side all at the same pace. Have you ever tried to walk over a stream at full gait on a single, skinny, slippery little pole? Each time we crossed a stream, Chief Fernando put an extra five steps between us.

At one point the chief raised his long machete and slashed angrily at the rain clouds overhead. Was he attempting to chase the clouds away, or was he angry with us for slowing him down? We heard the soft sound of approaching rain in the distance, coming steadily closer until rain began to pelt on the leafy canopy above. Strange, rain could penetrate where sunlight was held at bay. The trail became muddier and the logs more slippery.

The sun was just sinking behind the trees when we arrived at La Sabana. As I rubbed the muscles in the back of my legs, I gained an early respect for the people of the jungle. The Muinanes were a hardy people.

Stan and I slept that night in a small, split-palm storage/guest house about fifteen feet from Chief Fernando's *maloka*. Thankfulness, excitement, and bewilderment all seemed to overwhelm me. We had come to translate God's Word for a people who had never seen their language written. I wanted to sit and contemplate the meaning of it all—the mysteries of God's will and purpose—but it was no use. The two-day walk had been physically exhausting, and my thoughts were simple as I drifted off to sleep:

I may not have a blueprint of this jungle, but there is a map . . . and it is God's.

CHAPTER TWO

The Beginning of Dreams

Have patience with everything unresolved in your heart and try to love the questions themselves as if they were locked rooms or books written in a very foreign language. Don't search for the answers, which could not be given to you now, because you would not be able to live them. And the point is, to live everything. Live the questions now. Perhaps then, someday far in the future, you will gradually, without even noticing it, live your way into the answer.
— Rainer Maria Rilke in *Letters to a Young Poet*

JIM'S STORY
I awoke to the sound of birds, though their songs were quite different from any I had ever heard in Minnesota. I stretched carefully, grimacing slightly as my muscles reminded me of the two-day trek I had just completed.

Although I was eager to begin my first day in La Sabana, I listened for a few moments to the sounds of the jungle. Would I soon hear the sounds of my children playing here? Above my head, I noticed the beautiful, intricate weave of the leaf roof. How was God going to weave us into the Muinane culture? We couldn't just say we were coming; we would need permission. Why should they say yes? Why did Jan and I even want to come here, of all places?

La Sabana seemed to be beyond the farthest point of habitation. I had never felt so isolated, so far from anywhere, so cut off from everybody else in the world. But Jan and I were sure it was where God wanted us to be.

Why didn't God call us to more people? This was "poor economy" in the world's eyes. Maybe even some Christians quietly wondered if by putting resources into such a small tribe, they might not be neglecting a larger work, or perhaps their home endeavors.

The decision didn't make much sense to some people, and sometimes not even to us. But we aren't always able, in this life, to make sense out of everything that God does, for "the secret things belong to the Lord our God" (Deut. 29:29, NIV).

Why leave the ninety-nine and seek out the one — unless, of course, the one is me? Why leave heaven for earth? Why call fishermen and a tax collector to be your helpers? Why desert the crowds for one Ethiopian? Why bother with the small, the isolated, the despised? God's reasoning and God's ways are not our ways. God is always greater than our understanding.

I climbed out of my hammock and sat outside the doorway, in the morning light, to read from my New Testament. A few of the younger Muinanes, who had been to the mission school and knew some Spanish, asked if I would read in English and then tell them what it meant in Spanish. I read from the fourth chapter of 1 John. They

laughed at the strange sounds of English. As I explained
in Spanish, the words were familiar to some, but they
could not understand the meaning. Explaining intangible
concepts to the Muinanes would be difficult enough in
their own language. In a foreign tongue it would be
impossible. The Scriptures would have to be translated
into their own language.

One of the young men, perhaps twenty years of age,
was eyeing me strangely. He seemed interested, yet wary.

"What is your name?" I asked him in Spanish.

"I am Andrés, the oldest son of Chief Fernando," he
answered proudly. His smile faded as he pointed to my
New Testament and demanded, "What book is that?"

"It is the Bible," I responded.

"What is it about?"

"It's God's Word, and this book is one of the reasons I
want to come and live here. I want to learn your language
and someday translate this book for your people."

Like a good Muinane, Andrés tried to show no sign of
interest. But he looked at me intently, as if he wanted to
ask more questions. Then he turned and walked away.

When I met with Chief Fernando later that morning, I
told him I wanted to bring my family back to live in La
Sabana. He displayed no emotions, favorable or unfavor-
able. He said he would talk with the others. That night,
many came to talk about my proposal around the chief's
fire.

The next day I was told that Jan, the children, and I
could live with the Muinanes, but our house was to be
built on the other side of the Cahuinarí River.

The "village" of La Sabana was not really a village, at

least to our way of thinking. Four or five large family houses, called *malokas*, were scattered in the jungle, forty to ninety minutes apart. All except one were on the same side of the river. The only people who lived on the other side were the shaman, Manuel, and his wife, Cecilia. The Muinanes thought that only the shaman could appease and calm the evil spirits that presided there.

In the early 1900s the Peruvian rubber barons had set up one of their outposts on this site. The Muinanes had long ago destroyed every pole, every utensil, every trace of the "wicked Peruvians." Nothing remained but a two-hundred-acre grassy clearing, or *sabana*, that had been conceded to demonic spirits and the powers of hell. This is where my family was sent to live.

We needed an airstrip for our family to be flown in and out of the village. Knowing I could not bring my family over the two-day trail, we chose to make the airstrip first and then begin on our house, which would be located at the edge of the clearing just a hundred feet to the side of the runway.

The large grassy sabana made a natural airstrip. All we needed to do was cut the sabana grass, kick over some large termite nests, and clear approaches by felling some of the taller trees that blocked the ends of the sabana. Some of our colleagues in other parts of Colombia's jungles spent weeks and months cutting huge trees, pulling out mammoth stumps, filling holes, packing earth, and moving logs to make their airstrips. Had God placed the sabana at precisely the right spot in the jungle just for us?

I would like to hold to that thought, but I wonder if we don't too often have an inflated view of our importance in earth's history. Very few things are exclusively "just for me." God can and will do things specifically for each of us, but I wonder how often he must. Certainly not at my whim or demand! I may never know the others who are allowed to share "my special miracle"—or maybe it is I who share theirs.

This site hadn't always been a blessing. The sabana had supported some of the cruelest atrocities ever inflicted on a people, but soon it would facilitate the coming of light, life, and hope. Life is a mixture of marble and mud, the bitter and the sweet, death and life, sin and salvation.

Amid all the things I did not understand, I claimed that spot in the jungle as one of God's special provisions. Others may have abused, misused, and twisted any reason for its existence. Perhaps we, with God's help, could change things and make the sabana a place of blessing— at least for a time.

My second priority was to get a house started to which my family and I could return. Before leaving the Loma-linda center, I had talked with a fellow missionary who was a builder. I knew I couldn't construct the house without the help of the Indians. I also knew I would not have time to oversee the building of the whole house during that first survey trip.

"Don't worry," the builder told me. "You only need to make sure of one thing: The foundation must be square. After that, with the villagers' help, things will go up pretty much as they should. Just be sure the building is laid out square."

Good advice for houses and for lives. Get the foundation right before you begin. The missionary builder then showed me how to find the four corners, measure the diagonals, and square up the foundation. With this information, and with Stan's help, I felt confident as we began.

While Muinane men cut and carried large support poles from the jungle, I marked out the four corners of the house—measuring and remeasuring, checking and rechecking diagonals to be sure the corner poles would be set in the right spots. I also kept an eye on the Muinanes. This was my first opportunity to see their culture in action, and what I saw was quite different than the American way.

The Muinane society is a collective rather than an individualistic society. If one household is successful in hunting, the heavy beat of the signal drums carries the message: "We have meat; we have killed the wild pigs. Come, come."

Success is not measured so much for the individual as for the family and the community. Individual worth is measured by what he or she contributes to the group. Success in hunting, education, or economic gain is sought, not so much for personal advancement, but to be able to contribute more to one's family or community.

In contrast, we were from an individualistic society that placed high value on personal accomplishments. Often a group or organization has worth only as it relates to and contributes to our individual goals and successes. I quickly realized that we would need to make appropriate and significant adjustments in our behavior patterns. If we were to be successful in relating the gospel in this new context, we would need to establish a pattern of behavior that would be culturally appropriate to the Muinanes.

As I watched them working that day, I began to see that when building a house, preparing for a harvest dance, or making a canoe, the Muinanes assign each person a specific task. For example, one does not simply go into the jungle, cut a tree, and make a canoe. Making a canoe is a community project, and others need to be involved. As meat from a successful hunt is shared, so work is shared. Each is assigned a specific task. The men locate the right tree, which must meet many requirements. While some men cut down the tree, the women and children clear a path to the river. Other men cut limbs from smaller trees, placing them across the path. This forms a "road" over which the canoe-trunk is dragged on its way to the river. While some of the men and boys drag and push the tree, others are assigned to pick up the logs after the canoe-trunk passes and place them in the path ahead. This method of advancing the canoe over the same logs means that only a few logs are needed to drag a canoe log a great distance. When they finally reach the river, everyone rejoices as the huge log plummets down the steep embankment and crashes into the water.

When we were ready to translate Paul's writings in Romans and Corinthians, the Muinanes were already prepared to accept the truth. They thought it only natural and right that "we have many members in one body, and all members have not the same office: So we, being many, are one body in Christ, and every one members one of another (Rom. 12:4-5).

Back at my house, as the men arrived from the jungle with the twenty-foot poles on their shoulders, I hurried to point out exactly where each pole was to be set. I had done my homework; I had measured carefully; my house would be square. But I had forgotten one important factor: the chief.

When building a house, the chief is both head architect and supervisor. He decides where the house is to be built and who is assigned what job. He has full control over the decision-making process. Chief Fernando watched patiently, and I am sure with interest, as I explained where I had decided the poles were to be set. When I finished, the chief ordered some of the men to lift the four corner poles and stand each one upright. Stepping back a few yards, he studied the four poles and then, slowly waving his hand, he indicated that the far pole was to be moved a little to the left—no, too far . . . back a bit more—and the pole at the other corner just a little to the right. . . .

The chief had spoken; that's where the holes were dug and that's where the poles were set into the ground. I felt sick. All my planning, all the time spent learning how to "square up" a house, all my careful calculations seemed wasted. But I knew I was a guest. I was the outsider. I had come to fit into their culture, to serve them and not to be a lord over them. I was determined not to be the "ugly American." Outwardly, I was true to my determination; inwardly, I fumed. After I finally accepted that nothing could be done, I resigned myself to the fact that my family's house would not be square. We might as well move on with the rest of the building.

Everyone helped to carry split-palm bark for the raised floor and walls to the site. The women gathered a special kind of leaf, which would be woven onto long wooden palm strips to make huge shingles nine or ten feet long. These, in turn, would be hoisted and tied onto the roof with vines. By the time I returned with Jan and the children, the house would be ready for our little family to move into.

With the house started and the airstrip serviceable, I was eager to leave, get the family, and return. One of the items we had brought with us to La Sabana was a small, battery-powered radio transceiver. We had communicated daily with our Lomalinda center, and during the few weeks we were away, the Colombia Branch's first Helio Courier, Short Take Off and Landing (STOL) airplane had arrived. JAARS pilot Forrey Zander returned and circled the mission at La Chorrera, where he had last seen us starting off through the jungle behind the chief. With the thick green canopy below, he took a heading in the general direction of La Sabana.

He called on the plane's radio and asked how many hours we had walked. Did we change directions? Did we come near or notice any particularly high hills? They all seemed high when I was walking! Forrey was charting a new path over the jungle.

The Muinanes heard it first; then we heard the distant sound of the engine, to the north and west of us. "HK615, 615, this is Sabana. We can hear the engine. You are north and west of us. Do you copy? Over."

Forrey answered, "Tell someone to light a small fire." A few more minutes and Forrey saw the little clearing, checked the smoke from the fire for wind direction and velocity. He then buzzed low—very low—the full length of the airstrip, surveying length, width, surface, approaches, and whatever else a pilot does at a time like that.

We had done everything he asked us to do. I even checked the firmness of the surface by seeing how far I could push a machete blade into the ground. But Forrey knew if anything went wrong, we were a long, long way from anywhere! If I had been the pilot, would I have had the nerve to land an airplane on a brand-new jungle airstrip, constructed by two linguists? If anything went wrong, even if he survived a crash, the closest that the Aeronca seaplane could get was two days' walk away.

We all breathed a great sigh of relief when Forrey made a beautiful three-point landing, and the plane rolled to an immediate stop.

Before Stan and I left with Forrey, I wanted to check one more thing. I surreptitiously went back to measure the corners of my house. I wanted to know how far from square our home would be. I was surprised and humbled at what I found. The chief had done a wonderful job. Our home was almost perfectly square.

Could this be part of God's plan for us—that in order to minister to these people, we would have to humble ourselves, set aside our certainties in our own abilities? The chief was uneducated, superstitious, and believed that the earth was flat—and yet I would have to trust him for the safety and well-being of my wife and children. I would need to acknowledge my own insufficiency. I had to learn to trust the chief.

As I boarded the little plane, I turned to wave at the people who had gathered to see this strange flying machine. I was overcome with joy and excitement and thanksgiving. We had completed the survey to the Muinanes. We were ready to begin life with a group of people we prayed would accept us. By God's grace we hoped to be the agents through whom the Muinane tribe would also be represented in that "great multitude, which no man could number, of all nations, and kindreds, and people, and tongues" who will stand "before the throne, and before the Lamb, clothed with white robes, and palms in their hands," and who will cry, "Salvation to our God which sitteth upon the throne, and unto the Lamb" (Rev. 7:9-10).

We were ready to let a Lamb loose in the jungle.

CHAPTER THREE

First Impressions
and Close Encounters

If you came this way
Taking any route, starting from anywhere,
At any time or at any season,
It would always be the same:
You would have to put off
Sense and notion.
You are not here to verify,
Instruct yourself, or inform curiosity,
Or carry report. You are here to kneel
Where prayer has been valid. And prayer is more
Than an order of words, the conscious occupation
Of the praying mind, or the sound of the voice praying.
        —T. S. Eliot in "Little Gidding," *Four Quartets*

JAN'S STORY
While Jim was completing his initial survey, I was back
at Lomalinda with the children. I waited. I prayed. I worried. I prayed some more.

During the weeks before we left the States, our lives had been filled with activity. Then came language school, and our studies kept us busy. But I must be honest: The thrill had begun to wear off. Once the joy of committing ourselves to missions work led to the reality of selling all our possessions, once the farewell parties gave way to packing, and once the tearful good-byes no longer echoed in my ears, I began to see the implications of saying, "Yes, Lord."

I felt homesick, but for where? Our old home wasn't "home" anymore. I hadn't even seen La Sabana, didn't know for certain where our new home would be. We had shelter, but I felt homeless. And when you don't have a home, it is easy to feel that you don't have roots.

I didn't really doubt our calling, but I guess I did question the Lord a bit. *Are you sure this is where you want us? Can you promise me that my children will grow up unscathed by their experiences in the mission field? What if the Muinanes say no to our request? What if they say yes? Lord, do you realize that my entire world is changing?*

Each time I got discouraged, I felt God silently assuring me, *Your surroundings have changed, but your world has not. I was the Lord of life as you knew it, Jan, and I am the Lord of the jungle. I led you here. I will not leave you now.*

When Jim finally returned, he talked non-stop for hours. I watched his eyes dance as he spoke of the people and the possibilities. I saw genuine concern in his eyes as he told me about the people's needs and their hungers that went unsatisfied. Mostly, I saw his fierce determination and quiet resolution that this was, indeed, where God wanted us to be. And with certainty, I knew it, too.

For whatever reasons, this was God's plan. And I was thrilled and humbled to be a part of it.

On August 6, 1964, we all squeezed into the single engine Helio Courier with three hundred pounds of baggage: a radio, extra fuel for the airplane, bedding, some food, cooking utensils, hammocks, and clothes. We flew two and a half hours with nothing but the thick, impenetrable jungle below. We were less than an hour from La Sabana and the Muinanes when we ran into a terrible storm. With no alternate airfields, we had no choice but to turn around and go all the way back. We didn't want to go back; we wanted an option. This was our first encounter with how unfair and uncontrollable the jungle can be, and we didn't like the feeling.

After spending another night in Lomalinda, we left at nine o'clock the next day. Shortly after noon, we began looking for the little airstrip at La Sabana. I knew that at any moment, the trees would clear and we would see our new home. Suddenly, there it was—the airstrip and . . .

. . . a half-finished house. A wave of disappointment hit me when I realized that our little home was not even close to being finished. But I swallowed hard and regained my composure. We were here, and we were together. It was enough.

About fifteen women and children had arrived at the airstrip by the time we landed. They greeted us cautiously. Diana and Danny were afraid. I don't think they realized that the other children were scared too.

After we unloaded and refueled the plane, the chief came to tell us that we could stay in his storage/guest house until our house was ready. We graciously accepted his offer of the small room, which measured approximately nine-by-ten feet. We would have to cook over a fire in Chief Fernando's maloka.

Although we desperately wanted to be in our own home, this arrangement had its advantages. We learned a great deal by living directly with the chief and his family. The close contact furthered our language studies, allowed us to watch their society in action, and made us accessible to the people of the tribe. God turned our disappointment into a blessing.

Even so, many blessings in the jungle were mixed blessings, positive and not so positive. Until we moved to our new home, I had only one kettle to cook in, so we had only one dish at each meal. In the morning, it was oatmeal; in the evening, rice. We all got tired of this simple fare, but it gave me time to learn about cooking over an open fire on the floor.

We finally received one variation in the menu after the men took Jim hunting, but it wasn't exactly what I would have requested. I said I would never eat monkey, but in two weeks we'd had only one can of tuna and one can of wieners. Suddenly monkey meat seemed very appealing.

Shortly after we arrived, I wrote the following in a letter to our parents:

> We really enjoy the friendships we are developing. The children love it here. There is a girl, thirteen years old, who plays with them a lot. I enjoy visiting with the ladies; they are so interested in watching me curl my hair and Diana's. Theirs is very long and straight. By the way, please send us some pictures of

yourselves. The Muinanes are dying to know when you are coming here. One of the first questions they asked was, "Where are your parents?"

A Muinane family will all live together in a large house, called a maloka, and they are sure you will be coming as soon as they get our house built.

While writing this letter, I was interrupted by a pretty lady who came to visit. She asked what I was doing. I told her, "I'm writing to our mothers and fathers because we probably won't see them again for five years." She seemed extremely touched by this statement. Telling our parents about the conversation, I wrote:

Because the Muinanes live in extended family units, I don't think it will be hard for them to understand that it was no pleasure to leave our families far away in order to bring them the Word of Life. When they realize this, we think it will be a turning point. We continue to wonder who the first convert will be.

Ten days after our arrival, we had our first opportunity to witness about Christ through song. Andrés hooked up his radio to our antenna, and soon we heard gospel music in Spanish. Andrés said he liked music and asked me to sing in English. I sang "He Keeps Me Singing." Andrés' father and several others gathered around. We then listened to the rest of the fifteen-minute gospel broadcast.

Even those who knew some Spanish said they did not understand the meaning of what was being said. Jim told them that it would take time to learn their language, but someday we would give them books, hymns, and the Bible (New Testament) in Muinane. Our hearts filled with joy as we saw their faces light up. We prayed that we would be able to accomplish a great deal quickly.

Unfortunately, *quickly* is a relative term in the jungle. One of my journal entries during our first few weeks in La Sabana explains our frustration:

> *Aug. 19, 1964* — I'm sitting here with nothing important to do and feeling very lonely. We had an exciting welcome and lots of language help the first days, but now things have quieted down. The heavy part of building the house has come — putting down the floor. And now half of the men have had to leave La Sabana and go to help the rubber baron. There are only five men left here, and some of them have been sick. So *patience, patience* is needed each day.
>
> Jim and Andrés are working on the house and there isn't much opportunity for language study. I have little more opportunity as the women must go to the fields to get the bitter yucca root from which they make *casabe* bread for their families. They are gone from seven-thirty in the morning until two in the afternoon. When they get home with the yuca root, they work until dark — and sometimes into the night — squeezing out the poisonous liquid and preparing the root. This is the prime source of food. If the Muinanes use metaphors to any degree at all, they should have no problem understanding the force of Christ's claim, "I am the bread of life; he that cometh to me shall never hunger."

The "never hunger" part would also be important to the Muinanes. Some nights we heard Chief Fernando chanting to the gods for food. The people came to us asking for food, but we had not been able to bring much with us.

One of the foods the Muinanes did have was grub worms, purple and black worms that they boil and then eat. But the true delicacy to the Muinanes is the palm worm. Palm worms, which are large white grubs the size of a man's thumb, are "best" eaten uncooked and alive. In my journal I wrote, "I'm sure we won't be trying those for a while yet." I was wrong.

Fortunately, our first encounter with palm worms was in a dark maloka. I watched Jim closely as he chomped down on the worm. I doubt if anyone else noticed the look on his face, but I sure did. I quietly tossed my palm worm to one of the dogs lying in the shadows. No one saw me, thankfully, but I imagine they wondered why the dog suddenly liked me so much.

We dreaded the thought of having to eat another palm worm, but we felt that to be accepted, we must not demean their culture, traditions, homes, customs, or food. How could we tell them we didn't like something as "delicious" as palm worms? We prayed that, if we were offered another palm worm to eat, we would be gracious and would be able to get it down. We mostly prayed that such an offer would not come.

The first time we were invited to attend a Muinane celebration, we were not given palm worms. In fact, we were not given anything to eat. It was an early lesson on the interactive structure of the Muinane community, where everyone participates, and all who participate benefit.

We were told, "Bring your hammocks and come Saturday afternoon when the sun is just above the trees. There will be tribal dances and songs. People will come from every home, even some from distant villages. There will be an abundance of food, so much food you have never seen! The celebration will last through the night until the next day."

No one told us that all guests were to bring a gift of food. Each person arrived bearing gifts of peanuts, fruit, birds, smoked fish, meat, or live palm worms. These gifts were presented to the host. When the last gift was added to the growing pile of food, the celebration began.

Each gift was held high by the host, and the giver came forward. In return for the gift, he or she was given casabe bread, meat, and various fruits. The gift a person brought would be shared with others. Everything was carefully calculated and distributed. The size of a person's gift was considered, but it did not seem to be the primary consideration. Every man received enough to feed his family, no matter how large the family, or how much or how little he had brought. In the end, all the food was distributed to those who brought gifts.

We tried to look inconspicuous and unconcerned. Diana and Danny asked why we weren't eating when everyone else was. We tried to explain that this was new to us and we didn't understand the culture yet. We didn't know that we were supposed to bring a gift.

At first the Muinanes wondered if we had brought our own food, or maybe we didn't like their food. Why else would we have refused to bring a gift? It would have been impolite, in their culture, for them to accuse us by asking, and we sensed it would be wrong to ask for food when we had not brought a gift.

In the Muinane culture, those who do not participate by sharing do not receive. To the Western mind, this approach might seem unfair and even un-Christian. The Muinanes, of course, at that time did not claim the Christian faith. Even so, under the circumstances, we thought they were a little uncharitable; but we were wrong. The Muinane custom was, at its root, a biblical principle. The apostle Paul, writing to the Thessalonians, said, "For even when we were with you, this we commanded you, that if any would not work, neither should he eat" (2 Thess. 3:10). We were confusing American cultural ideas with biblical principles. We had much to learn, and to unlearn, if we were going to communicate the gospel cross-culturally.

Just as we were beginning to hope that Jim, Andrés, and the few men left in the village would be able to finish our home shortly, we ran into a greater obstacle. A man came across the trail to La Sabana with orders that all remaining men who were in debt to the rubber baron must be in Araracuara on August 25 and would not return until December or January. This included Andrés, who had accepted a transistor radio and other merchandise amounting to approximately 110 U.S. dollars. He would work fourteen hours a day for approximately four months to pay his debt to the rubber baron. This left us with no help for our house or language studies.

My frustration grew to a boiling point when Diana developed a fungus infection in her scalp from the mosquitoes and gnats. Even after treating it for a week, I still spent an hour and a half daily trying to wash her scalp and get rid of the infection. One of the little boys in the village had the same condition and was losing his hair. Naturally, I was frightened.

Then a huge blister appeared on Diana's thumb. After we had soaked it several times, it finally broke and began to bleed profusely. But the opening wasn't large enough, and Jim had to cut it with a razor blade and dig out the infection. Diana screamed for hours.

I wanted to scream, too. I was ready to give up. I told Jim that if our children had to suffer so much, I couldn't take it, and we would have to go home. But even as I said the words, I knew that God loved my children even more than I did. I simply had to learn to trust the Lord.

The big issue wasn't where we raised our kids and whether they faced the unfamiliar sicknesses of the jungle or the familiar sicknesses of the United States. As the years passed, we wouldn't care much about whether they slept in a hammock or a bed, or where they went to school. What we would care a great deal about is whether they loved us, would love their mates, would love their own children, and most of all, that they would know and love God. Everything else pales by comparison.

On September 14, we finally moved into our house. It wasn't finished yet—the ceiling over our bedroom and a few doors were still missing. But we felt that the time had finally arrived.

We were excited as we climbed the log ladder into our house. At first we felt a little tentative about the split-palm floor because it bounced as we walked across it. But we soon grew accustomed to the shaking and the knowledge that we were walking six feet above the ground. The walls were also constructed of split palm, which gave an illusion of privacy. But long vertical cracks in the palm floor and walls let in sights, sounds, smells, smoke, bugs and other small animals, and, of course, the ever-present gnats. But it was home, at last.

Our toilet was a path that ran into the jungle some distance from the back of the house. In the middle of the night, it required a good strong flashlight—as well as a lot of courage—to go down the steps and walk out into the jungle. We didn't worry about the large animals; we knew when they were around. The snakes scared us the most.

We caught rainwater to drink by stretching a large piece of plastic between two vines. If the plastic was hung right and the wind didn't blow, the water could be funneled to run into a small pail. This way we didn't have to boil water until the rainwater ran out.

We also gathered rain from the leaf roof of our house and funneled the water into a 120-gallon storage tank. Pipes ran from the tank to the kitchen sink and down under the house to a sprinkler head, which was our shower when we couldn't get to the river.

I thought the storage tank was a great idea until I opened the faucet and discovered more than water—a baby tree frog dropped into the sink. As long as the water in the tank was used up regularly, allowing the rains to replace the water, we experienced few difficulties. But water left in the tank too long would stagnate and putrefy very quickly. Mold, slime, tadpoles, frogs, cockroaches, spiders, and centipedes all found their way into the unused tank of water.

An open conduit or a fast-flowing stream will remain fresh and pure. But I soon learned that without springs feeding the body of water, and without sufficient outflow, the water will stagnate. As Christians, we must have fresh supplies of God's grace and goodness each day; we must be connected to the source. But we cannot shut ourselves off from the world, hoarding our blessings. "Whoso hath this world's good, and seeth his brother have need, and shutteth up his bowels of compassion from him, how dwelleth the love of God in him?" (1 John 3:17). We had come to the jungle with the mistaken idea that we were the teachers. We soon discovered how much we had to learn—from the Muinanes and from the Lord.

During our first night in our new home, I kept listening to the sounds of the jungle. Within weeks they became familiar, but that first night they were unnerving. While we were living next to the chief's maloka, we heard mostly human sounds. But on the other side of the river, alone, we heard the jungle noises:

- The low cooing of the dove, followed at dusk by the king *mochilero* (an oriole-like bird), calling hundreds of *mochileros* to the trees where they spent the night
- The whirring of beetle wings
- The almost silent *swish, swish* of the vampire bats
- The *whoo, whoo* of an owl, and the five beautifully descending notes of another
- The muffled growl of a jaguar as it passed along the edge of the sabana in search of food

- A rat scurrying across a ceiling pole
- A million crickets, bugs, and insects chirping
- The silence before the dawn, and then what
  seemed to be the roar of a waterfall or an approaching train, but was just the deafening
  chatter of howler monkeys waking up.

A few days later, as we were resting in our hammocks, Diana asked, "Daddy, what does *saved* mean?" In simple words, Jim told her the plan of salvation. When she was three, she had wanted Jesus to come into her heart, but we didn't think she truly understood. This time she seemed so certain as she asked, "Can I be saved now, Daddy?" Our daughter prayed, and we rejoiced.

We had come all the way to the Amazon jungle to bring the message of salvation to a small tribe of Indians. Yet our first convert was our own daughter.

CHAPTER FOUR

Earning Trust and Learning Faith

Nothing is small or great in God's sight;
Whatever he wills becomes great to us, however seemingly
*   trifling,*
And if the voice of conscience tells us that he requires
*   anything of us,*
we have no right to measure its importance.
On the other hand, whatever he would have us do,
however we think it, is as naught to us.
               —Jean Nicolas Grou

JIM'S STORY

When you hear someone you hardly know say, "Trust me," is your first inclination to do the opposite? If you have ever been swindled, cheated, or lied to—or even know someone who has—you learn not to trust indiscriminately. You tend to be more cautious, perhaps even suspicious, if someone you don't know acts too nice.

Imagine our challenge with the Muinanes. They had been the victims of some of the cruelest atrocities known to humankind. They had suffered greatly at the hands of outsiders; and here we were, asking them to trust more outsiders. Thus, one of our primary goals during those first months at La Sabana was earning the people's trust. Acceptance would require years of loving and caring for them and their children in practical ways. We knew we could never minister to them if they did not have faith in us. We didn't know that *our* faith would also grow in the process.

Less than a month after our arrival, we received one of our first opportunities to increase their faith in us—and our faith in God. It was also our first chance to use the limited medical training we received at Wycliffe's Jungle Training Camp in Mexico.

At five-thirty in the afternoon, four women came down the trail to Chief Fernando's *maloka*. A young woman in her midtwenties was carrying her mother on her back. She had walked an hour through the jungle—climbing steep hills and crossing streams on single poles used as bridges, all the while carrying her mother piggyback style. As they passed by the chief's guest house where we were staying, the mother appeared to be in shock. Fifteen minutes later they called for us, asking if we could do anything to help.

Death seemed close. Her eyes were rolling, and her low moans were drowned out by the chattering of her teeth. As those around began wailing, we asked someone to help translate since we, as yet, knew only greetings in Muinane. We were told that over an hour earlier she had begun vomiting violently and had diarrhea. She had eaten an animal, but the others had eaten the same animal. They insisted that I treat her.

I wanted to help, but I wasn't about to treat her unless

I knew everything that happened. Obviously, it wasn't the meat, or someone else would be sick. Did she eat anything else? Drink something? They all looked at us sheepishly, then looked at each other, but no one wanted to talk.

When Chief Fernando finally arrived, I asked him to find out exactly what had transpired. As the chief spoke to the woman, he felt her hip. Then he turned and quietly said, "This is Regina. She thinks she was bitten by a *bujelia.*"

I looked at Jan, but she only shrugged her shoulders in return. Was *bujelia* a Muinane or Spanish word? It sounded somewhat like the Spanish word *brujeria,* which means witchcraft, but I had no way of knowing if that's what the chief meant. So I asked the obvious question. "What's a bujelia?"

They hesitated, but someone finally said, "It's an animal that walks around at night and sneaks into houses to bite people. After three days, the person dies."

Then I asked what must have seemed to them the dumbest question of all. "Can you describe it better, or draw me a picture?"

We were expecting them to describe a jaguar, spider, poisonous liquid, or something else we could identify. When they looked at me as if I were crazy, I suddenly realized my interpretation had been correct. How could they draw witchcraft? They assumed we understood the powers and forces of the spirit world and that witchcraft is feared, not explained.

Unable to get any further information, I finally insisted that they carry the ailing woman outside the dark *maloka* so I could examine her hip in the last ray of daylight.

What I saw spurred me into action: two small puncture wounds about a half-inch apart. Snakebite! Jan helped me give Regina an injection of antivenin, and we prayed that it wasn't too late.

She vomited once in the night and had terrible pain. In the morning she couldn't see. We helped them prepare a banana drink, told them to give her plenty of liquids, and shared the few aspirin and vitamins that we had. And we prayed some more. We prayed that Regina would get well and survive her snakebite. We prayed that God would use her illness to help us earn the people's trust. Mostly, we prayed that the Muinanes would soon find light and life in Christ, and that they would be free from the fear of unknown spirits and evil curses.

Our petitions turned to thanksgiving when, by the evening of the second day, Regina regained her sight. She was on the road to recovery. And we were on our way to a solid relationship with the Muinanes.

The one person most likely to oppose our presence in La Sabana was the shaman, Manuel. We had heard many stories of shamans who perceived outside help as a threat to their power and influence in the tribe—especially when it came to medical help. Although some shamans are considered evil, sending only curses and death, Manuel was considered a good shaman. Manuel helped people get well. We did not know how he would react to the people's requests for our medicine.

Manuel and Cecilia lived on the same side of the river as our family, but we seldom saw them. They lived twenty minutes away, and they seldom left their maloka, concerned that they might miss someone who was in need. People went to Manuel when they were oppressed by demons or fearful of a curse. They came to talk and seek advice. But mostly they came to be healed.

Then Manuel became critically ill. Someone carried the old man across the river to Chief Fernando's maloka, where he lost consciousness. We were not advised until things became desperate, when Cecilia came back across the river to our house. "Manuel is dying," she cried. "Please come and bring your medicine. You must save him!"

I had read stories in missionary biographies about this type of experience—the kind of opportunity I half-expected to happen because it seems that's the way God should work in primitive environments. Still, when it happened to me in the middle of the Amazon jungle, I also felt a twinge of fear and doubt. *God, you are doing this, aren't you? Manuel is going to get better, isn't he? God, do you realize what will happen if I treat him and he dies?*

I took a small bag of medicines while Jan stayed with the children and prayed. When I arrived at Chief Fernando's maloka, I approached the shaman's hammock and listened to his breathing. He had a great deal of congestion, a fever, and other symptoms pointing to a severe respiratory infection and pneumonia. I gave him an injection of penicillin, prayed, and left some packaged soup mixes before returning home.

The waiting was torture. In spite of my faith, I wondered what would happen to us if the shaman died. Would I be blamed? Manuel was well loved and trusted, and I was so new. Would we even be permitted to stay?

As usual, all my worrying was unnecessary. Within a

few days, Manuel was out of his hammock and ready to go home. Before he left, he stopped by our house and said, "Jim, my spirit had left me, but you brought it back. I owe you very much."

I realized in that moment how much I owed the Lord. I was working hard to develop the Muinanes' faith in me so they could ultimately believe what I told them about God. But God seemed equally as concerned about my faith in him. I was learning to trust the Lord in ways I had never imagined.

Manuel became a close friend, and as time went on we noticed that more Muinanes were coming to us for medical help. Both the white man's medicine and the jungle herbs were revered. There was no competition, no struggle to replace one with the other, but rather a growing respect for the effectiveness of both modern and traditional medicines. One day a man confided, "I went to see Manuel first, and he told me to come see you because he said, 'Jim's medicine is stronger than mine.'"

The Muinanes came to us with colds, fevers, scorpion stings, eye infections, skin infections, and arthritis. They came with anemia, diarrhea, amoebas, worms, parasites, and machete cuts. One man came with a badly mangled foot: He had stepped into a pool of water and right into the mouth of an alligator. Our knowledge and resources were limited; we could only treat the ailments to alleviate pain and ward off infection.

Once when our food supply was low, Manuel brought us a large jungle bird. In cleaning the bird we found a beautiful green-shelled egg. It reminded us of a colored Easter egg. Later that day we were told that the chief's

wife, Alicia, had unknowingly drunk a poison being prepared to poison fish. We talked to the doctor at
Lomalinda via radio (as we so often did) to consult with
him regarding medical treatment.

"Give her the uncooked whites of chicken eggs," he
advised. We didn't have chickens at the time, but we did
have an egg—the beautiful green-shelled "Easter" egg
carried to us inside a bird, by Manuel. Alicia recovered.
God's footprints were everywhere.

Inevitably, there came a situation that required emergency measures that far exceeded our abilities. Thankfully, they did not exceed God's. A Huitoto family was
passing through La Sabana when their nine-year-old son
jumped over a log and fell on a pointed stick. The stick
entered near the groin area and was driven six to eight
inches into the boy's body, near the surface. When the
parents pulled the stick out, it broke, leaving about an
inch and a half in the abdomen area. We could feel the
end of the broken stick but could not determine how far
below the surface it lay. We knew this was far beyond
our limited medical/health training, and the nearest doctor was at the national penitentiary in Araracuara.

We made contact on our radio-transceiver and asked
for a plane to come from Lomalinda, not knowing how
we would pay for the boy's flight. Our account would be
charged for the flight, and we didn't have the money. But
this was an emergency.

We wanted to ask for extra help from the churches and
friends at home who supported us. But we had no way of
contacting them; and even if we did, the money would
arrive much later than the bill.

A month later we returned to Lomalinda and saw our financial statements. The month when we were charged for the boy's emergency flight, an extra three hundred dollars in support was sent to us from people at home. How did they find out? Only God knows, for they had responded to the inner voice from God and sent their gifts *before* the boy fell on the stick. We hoped that through this experience, the Muinanes would witness our compassion and love. All we saw was the miraculous working of God.

Of all the things we were called upon to do, the one that I most disliked was dentistry. Dentists have my highest admiration. From the very beginning, I decided that I would give injections, hand out pills, dress wounds, and anything else I was capable of doing, but "Don't ask me to pull teeth!" I consoled myself that the Muinanes could get their teeth pulled in La Chorrera, which was only two days' walk from La Sabana, or in Araracuara, three or four days away.

Then old Magdalena came to me with a toothache, swollen mouth, and fever. I was not prepared for this. If I pulled an abscessed tooth, the infection could spread. I would have to give her antibiotics whether I pulled the tooth or not. Hadn't I warned them that they should get any bad teeth taken care of before this happened?

"Magdalena, you should have taken care of this at La Chorrera! I will give you something for the pain and infection, but you need to go get the tooth pulled."

"No, my son, *you* are going to pull my tooth!"

"You don't understand. I have nothing for the pain and I have no pliers. You need to go where they can help you."

But Magdalena, as usual, was insistent. "I am old, and I will die on the trail. I will also die if this tooth is not removed. I know you have pliers; I have seen them."

I was starting to sweat. "No! Those are not the kind of pliers you can pull teeth with; they're for fixing things. And without an injection to numb your mouth, it will hurt too much!"

"Jim, you *must* pull my tooth, or I will have to look for a nail or a knife and try to pry it out. But if I do, it will get infected, just as you are always warning us. Then I will die for sure."

She sure knew how to pile on the guilt! I finally realized I had little choice. I thought it would be an easy tooth to pull since Magdalena had few remaining teeth and it stood pretty much alone. I asked Jan to pray that neither the tooth nor I would break. It didn't come out as easily as I expected. Magdalena screamed, and my wrist became weak; the more she screamed, the weaker I became. I stopped. It was no use: I didn't have the right tools or the fortitude. I was afraid I would crush the crown and leave a piece of the root. I had nothing to give her for the pain.

But Magdalena begged, "Jim, listen to me. You're going to try again. It's going to hurt, and I'm going to scream. But you are going to pull my tooth. When I scream, don't listen to me. You just keep pulling and don't stop until the tooth is out!"

That was the first tooth I pulled. As more people came to me for help, it became evident that I could no longer hide from my responsibility to help when I could. This was the jungle, and there were no alternatives.

I decided that if I was going to pull teeth, I was going to learn what I could and get the right tools. A dentist in Minnesota helped provide elevators, extractors, and anesthesia. Friends helped me locate illustrated dental textbooks. A Colombian dentist invited me to visit a prison in Bogotá, where I watched and learned about dry sockets and the importance of injecting anesthesia slowly.

Dentistry became a little easier with the proper instruments and some knowledge of what might lie beneath the gums. I was also reassured that it wasn't strength, but technique and rotation that were most important in the extraction of a tooth. I'm sure that is true, but no matter how much I studied the illustrations and rotation techniques, my wrists would go limp as soon as I looked into a person's mouth.

I guess God figured the Muinanes and I had all suffered enough, because after several years he gave me an assistant. A young man named Arturo became fascinated with dentistry when I removed his daughter's tooth. Whenever I was going to pull somebody's tooth, he came to watch. I seized my opportunity. At first Arturo watched while I explained what I was doing. Then he helped me. Ultimately, Arturo pulled the teeth and I watched. At last I was out of a job: I was no longer the local dentist. My involvement in dentistry was then limited to encouraging the Muinanes to care for their teeth and explaining how they could prevent tooth decay. Real dentistry still had to be done in La Chorrera or Araracuara, where there was electricity and equipment. But emergency tooth extraction could be safely done by Arturo, and it could be done whether or not we were there.

Jan and I thought it was important to train the people and empower them to help themselves rather than teaching them to be dependent upon us. The old adage is true: Give a man a fish, and you feed him for a day; teach a man to fish, and you feed him for a lifetime. We wanted to be teachers.

From our very first days with the Muinanes, we were sadly aware of the scarcity of food, especially foods with protein. Although food was sometimes simply scarce, the root of the problem rested on the division of labor, which is well defined among the Muinanes. Only the men hunt and fish. They also must cut and burn the fields to prepare them for the next year's planting. This, of course, means that when the men aren't around, the food supply is dangerously limited.

And the men were gone frequently. Most Muinane men had accepted trade goods from a rubber baron in Araracuara. When the baron sent messengers over the trail, the Muinanes were required to go work off their debt. But before they could pay off their debt, they would accept more trade goods and food items. Each time, they built up an even larger debt, leaving them permanently indebted. Most of the Muinane men were required to spend a large part of the year away from La Sabana, their families, and their gardens.

When we arrived in the village, we found poor gardens and no meat. We were not agriculturists, though Jan knew more than I since she had grown up on a dairy farm. We had not come as doctors, dentists, technicians, or community development workers; we were Bible translators and linguists. But we couldn't ignore their needs.

Someday we would translate the book of James, which says, "Suppose a brother or sister is without clothes and daily food. If one of you says to him, 'Go, I wish you well; keep warm and well fed,' but does nothing about his physical needs, what good is it?" (James 2:15-16, NIV). How could they believe in God if we hadn't shown them God's compassion?

Becoming involved was not easy. Many of our attempts at community development were failures. But the Muinanes expressed their needs, and we learned together what worked and didn't work for them at the time.

They asked for chickens, so chickens became our first village project. We needed a bird that would give good egg production, was meaty, and could survive the jungle climate. We were told that most good laying hens wouldn't sit on their eggs. We needed eggs, but we also needed to hatch some of the eggs to insure the ongoing success of the venture. We finally decided to start with a few Rhode Island Reds and to bring along a "jungle incubator." Our "incubator" was a hardy, run-of-the-mill, country chicken that wasn't very big and didn't lay many eggs, but would allow us to slip the larger eggs into her nest. She hatched brood after brood of Rhode Island Red chicks.

We didn't have the resources to give every family some chickens, and it was unacceptable to give chickens to only one family. So we began with a few chickens of our own. As we built the flock, we hoped to demonstrate that chickens could survive and produce in La Sabana. When the flock was larger, we would give a few starter birds to each household.

When the flock was just beginning to increase nicely,

we had to leave to go to our mission center at Lomalinda. We asked one family to care for the small but growing flock. When we returned to La Sabana, only a rooster and a few hens were still alive. We were told that the jaguars had eaten the fat hens. Others whispered that it was really "people-jaguars" that had eaten the hens. We never found out, but we began again to build the flock in order that we might someday give each household a few hens, a rooster, and another hen for hatching.

Caring for chickens in the jungle wasn't easy, but in an area where wild game was becoming increasingly hard to find, it was a welcome supplement to their diet. Over the years, the Muinanes never seemed to let their little flocks of chickens get very large before they would eat one. But always they were able to gather a few eggs, enjoy some meat, and keep one or two chickens for a time of greater need.

The success of the chicken project stimulated the Muinanes' interest in trying to raise other domesticated animals. We wish we could say that we were the ideal intercultural-development workers. We wish we could list all successes, or at least, mostly successes. In contrast to the traditional role of developers, we wanted to become facilitators.

Facilitating meant understanding how their culture differed from our own so that our projects would be appropriate for their societal needs. As we were able to identify and compare our own cultural values to those of the Muinane culture, we saw that their cultural values were different, but they were not wrong. Their values match those listed by L. R. Kohls in his study of world values, which reveals that Americans differ in basic values with seven-eighths of the world (L. R. Kohls, *Survival Kit for Overseas Living: for Americans planning to live and work abroad* [Yarmouth, Maine: Intercultural Press, 1984], pp. 4–16). He noted, for instance, that Americans are more interested in *change* while other countries value *tradition;* Americans value *control over one's environment,* others leave their circumstances to *fate;* and Americans value *competition,* while others honor *cooperation.*

The differences in values held by us and those of other cultures directly affect the programs we seek to implement. These cultural values are neither right nor wrong; they are merely different. We were determined not to seek to homogenize the world by degrading other cultures and traditions.

On the other hand, some moral and ethical values are right and others are wrong. C. S. Lewis distinguished between cultural values, "conventions," and moral values, which he calls "real truths."

> We learn the rule of Decent Behavior from parents and teachers, and friends and books, as we learn everything else. But some of the things we learn are mere conventions which might have been different. We keep to the left of the road, but it might just as well have been the rule to keep to the right—and others of them, like mathematics, are real truths. (Lewis, C.S., *Mere Christianity,* [New York: Macmillan, 1952], pp. 6, 10)

Ethical and moral accountability must be measured by an absolute standard, or ultimately there is no basis for accountability. If there is a shifting standard of ethics, at times injustice will be permitted and evil accepted as good. Similarly, it is at this point where some Christians stumble. If we confuse moral and ethical values with cultural values, we will fail to understand that some values, or conventions, function at a different level of significance, and yet they are very much a part of a society's functioning.

If we had done a better job of understanding these issues while with the Muinanes, we might have had fewer failures and more successes. Nevertheless, we did the best we could, and we believe that is what God requires.

We were forewarned of the problems that come with pigs, but the Muinanes were most eager to have pigs. The wild pigs migrated close to the village less frequently, and the Muinanes thought it would be great to have pork as available as chicken. We agreed to help, but asked that they agree to certain conditions. First, they would build a pen so the pigs would not run wild near the houses, increasing the danger of hookworm. They would plant sweet yuca to feed the pigs. We would give one family two pigs, and from the first litter, they would give a pair to another family, and so on.

The pigs got out and into a neighbor's garden. It was hard for the Muinanes to understand why they should raise food to feed an animal that might die tomorrow or be eaten by a jaguar. The pigs became sick; the litters were small and most died. The owners were getting nothing in return for their work, and there were no piglets to pass on to the next household. Fights ensued, and the whole project was a miserable failure.

Later came the goats—they ate everything, including clothes and the thatch roofs of the houses; African long-haired sheep didn't adjust to the jungle; and even the cattle and rabbits were failures. The only benefit from these experiments was that we became part of the community and part of their struggle to "improve."

As bungling and unsuccessful as many of the projects were, our responding to their requests, our struggling and our failing with them, demonstrated that we wanted to be a part of their lives, their families, and their community. Perhaps, because we tried, they accepted our help.

If we were to start over today, we would do many things differently. But some things we would not change. We would still seek to help, and we would want the people to determine their own needs. We would try to be responsive to the needs they expressed, and at the same time, be more alert to sense their obvious unspoken needs. Most of all, we would love them, just as we did.

We weren't perfect, but perfection is not what God requires. God rewarded our efforts, both in external and internal ways. So the pigs ate everything in sight! So our every effort wasn't a rip-roaring success. In the long run, in the eternal view, what matters?

One thing that matters is this entry in Jan's journal on January 16, 1968, almost four years after arriving in La Sabana: "Manuel and Cecilia trusted Christ today!"

We prayed for an increase in the Muinanes' faith; we received an increase in our own. We prayed for success in our efforts; the glorious events were all God's doing.

The shaman said to me, "I owe you very much."

We repeat the same words to our Savior. "Jesus, we owe you very much."

CHAPTER FIVE

Intersecting Miracles

*With meekness, humility, and diligence, apply yourself to
the duties of your condition. They are seemingly little things
which make no noise that do the business.*
—Henry More

JIM'S STORY
In the United States, most of us are familiar with the
pleasures and pains of blended families. Stepchildren and
stepparents add a unique mix to the family unit. But if
you think these situations are challenging, you should
have met Chief Fernando's family.

Chief Fernando's first wife gave birth to Andrés and several daughters. When Fernando remarried, she left the village, taking her children with her. His second wife was
rejected because "she could not give him sons." Then came
Alicia, Fernando's third wife. She chased the second wife
out of the maloka with a machete, and no one in the tribe
ever saw or heard from the chief's second wife again.

At least two of Alicia's children had been killed or left
to die. One of the babies cried incessantly and was stran-

gled after a week. Another was buried alive, as he evidently had a harelip. They said, "His mouth didn't serve."

You might be asking what kind of savages these people are, that they would kill their own children. But history may prove them no more savage or brutal than we. When death and violence in any culture are frequent and commonplace, they become easily accepted. While the Muinanes deal with unwanted babies in their primitive ways, often in the United States our own clinically cruel ways of ridding ourselves of unwanted babies show that we have no cause to throw stones.

The Muinanes had never known release from fears, jealousy, mistrust, darkness, and superstitions; these were the basis for killing some of their newborn babies. They had never known the Good News of Jesus Christ and had not recognized the love of God. The jungle was the only teacher they had ever known, and it could be harsh and cruel. Death is common; only the strongest survive.

The Muinanes have no hospitals and no private rooms in their houses. When it comes time for a Muinane woman to give birth, she will find a long knife or even a machete, and a piece of cloth if it is available. She will then walk five to ten minutes into the jungle. If her mother or grandmother is in the *maloka,* she may ask one of them to go along to help cut the umbilical cord and clean the baby before returning. Often, however, the girl or woman will go to the jungle alone. She cuts a large plantain leaf to place on the ground and squats to deliver her baby. She must cut the cord, which she then ties with a string of *cumari,* palm fiber. She carries her baby back to the *maloka* and lies down in her hammock near the fire.

Alicia went alone to the jungle to give birth to her third child. As she walked, knife in hand, down the jungle trail, she may have thought of the child whose "mouth didn't serve." Perhaps she wondered if the baby would be good, unlike the baby who cried incessantly. Or maybe she thought of Fernando's warning that he did not want another girl.

Alicia, feeling the sharp pangs of birth, squatted above the plantain leaf, and soon a baby dropped to the earth. What should have been a moment of joy and relief became a horrible realization—the baby was a girl! Alicia picked up the knife and cut the umbilical cord. Then she started the agonizing walk back through the jungle to the *maloka,* her fire, and her hammock. She left the child on the jungle floor, to die or to be eaten by a wild animal.

The baby's grandmother, Magdalena, realized that Alicia had returned from the jungle alone and went to search for the baby. Picking the child up from the jungle floor, she pulled a handful of leaves from a nearby tree and cleaned up the baby. She returned and insisted that Alicia nurse the hungry girl. Magdalena's granddaughter was named Clementina.

We met Clementina shortly after our arrival in La Sabana. She was a barefooted eleven-year-old with dark, straight hair and black eyes—eyes that watched us with amusement as we tried to carry water up the hill from the river.

The Muinanes need the river for food, transportation, and especially for water. Because rivers may rise twelve to twenty feet overnight, the people build their houses on the top of a hill, high above the river. We were young, but the river was three hundred yards away, straight down—and, of course, straight back up.

We carefully inched our way down the steep footpath—unless it rained, and then we would fall, slip, slide, and crash our way to the water's edge, and beyond. We would fill the bucket with river water and face an even greater challenge—returning to the top of the hill. We arrived covered from front to back with red mud, carrying by then only half a bucket of water.

After watching us for a while, Clementina offered to carry our water from the river. My pride and male ego were challenged. I had the same feeling as when a grocery checkout girl in the States would offer to carry my groceries to the car. I realized, however, that by continuing to carry the water, I would do little more than provide the Muinanes with slapstick comedy twice a day, and in addition we would never have quite enough water.

I wondered if my hesitancy was because I feared the reaction of other Americans, who might hear that we paid an eleven-year-old girl to carry water for us. But Jan had her hands full with cooking over an open fire, washing clothes at the river, and caring for two young children in the Amazon jungle. I went every day with men of the tribe to build our house on the other side of the river. We were finding it increasingly difficult to help with medical needs, begin disciplined language analysis, learn about the culture, or even reach out in love to share God's message with those we came to minister to. If we were going to help the Muinanes, we would have to let them help us. So Clementina, for the reward of helping someone in need and for a few cents, carried water for the strange outsiders.

Clementina spent the next five years attending the Roman Catholic boarding school in La Chorrera, where we first flew into the jungle. During those years, we saw her only during her breaks from school, but our friendship with the girl continued to grow. Because of her excellent grades, she was chosen to attend a parochial secondary school in Leticia, where she studied to become a teaching assistant.

In 1969, after spending the Christmas school break with Diana and Dan at Lomalinda, we returned to La Sabana while Clementina was still at home. Clementina, who was almost sixteen, offered to help Jan with work around the house. In only a few days she would leave again for school, but Clementina seemed eager to work and be near us, even for the few remaining days. She was a wonderful helper, assisting Jan with cooking on the mud stove, washing clothes at the river, and checking entries in our dictionary file.

What did washing, cooking, and cleaning have to do with real missionary work? The Bible has much to say about the ordinary things of daily living. Our dictionary file quickly grew with words and concepts we would later need for "the washing of regeneration," the bread of life, a lump of dough, and leaven.

As Jan and Clementina worked side by side, Clementina answered Jan's questions about the language. In return, Clementina asked Jan questions about the Bible. Three days before she was to return to school, Clementina prayed with Jan and asked Christ to wash away her sin and create a clean heart within her.

Over the next few years, Clementina finished her schooling and then taught kindergarten at the primary school in La Chorrera. All the while, she read the Bible and fell increasingly in love with the Scriptures and with her Savior.

At twenty years of age, Clementina announced to us that God was calling her to go to Bible college. We tried to warn her of all the problems. Her jungle schooling had totaled only about seven years, and she had not yet completed high school. We explained that the Bible school was an evangelical school, and that the other students would likely have had years of evangelical training in their churches while Clementina's exposure to evangelical Christianity and its teachings was very new. The language barrier was another problem because the teaching would be in Spanish; she understood Spanish fairly well, but she would be at a definite disadvantage to those who were studying in their native tongue. And last, but certainly not least, she had no money to pay for her schooling.

She was single-minded in her purpose, and her response to our well-intentioned warnings was simple. "But Jim, God wants me to go to Bible school. I'll save what I can. I'll sew little dresses and maybe people will buy them for their children. I can clean houses. God wants me to go to Bible school, and I'm sure he will help me."

We didn't argue further, but we knew it could never be. Then Clementina was accepted at the Christian and Missionary Alliance Bible School in Armenia, Colombia. God had answered Clementina's prayers.

She did struggle with the Spanish language. She wrote, "It is very hard here. They talk about doctrine and theology and it is very hard to understand these things in the Spanish language. Many nights, I have to also study somewhere else to complete my high school studies. I study most of the night, every night, trying to keep up. The Bible school requires us to take Greek, and that's even harder for me than Spanish."

Hadn't we warned her? What were we thinking of, letting a Muinane girl from the Amazon jungle pursue such a foolhardy idea?

But the Lord gave her good rapport with her teachers and the other students. She was given a scholarship for the second semester and ended the year on the honor roll. It wasn't easy, considering the language barrier, cultural conflicts, and spiritual warfare that could be traced back to her early life with demonic conflicts in the tribe. But she was making it—and even doing well.

During her second year at the Bible school, she met a wonderful young Colombian national and fellow student. She and Edgar Buenaventura were married a year before they graduated from the four-year program. Clementina became the first Indian—and the first woman—to finish all four years and graduate from the Bible school.

Clementina and Edgar, along with their two children, now serve as volunteers with SIL in Colombia. After completing two linguistic courses in preparation for translation, they worked for a time with the Guayabero and Macaguan tribes. They served in many capacities at SIL's Lomalinda Center and are presently blessing the lives of many missionaries in Colombia. They are assigned as translators and have begun translating God's Word for the Achagua tribe.

God saved the life of a baby girl who was supposed to die. That girl became a woman and is now bringing life in the name of Jesus Christ to those who might die without the Good News. Whenever we think of Clementina, we rejoice in God's goodness and the wonders of God's plan. And we also remember.

We remember another young girl who "should have died"—or at least everyone feared that she would. She was born fifteen years before Clementina and lived thousands of miles from the jungle, in the little farming community of Humboldt, Iowa.

The girl's father, the son of a Danish immigrant pastor, worked long hours at the local creamery. His wife, Ruth, rose early, long before daylight, to wash clothes in boiling lye water before her children woke up. One morning the little girl awoke early, wandered into the kitchen to see what her mommy was doing, and fell backwards into the tub of scalding lye water. She was instantly burned over much of her body, and her skin was pulled from her body as her parents peeled off her pajamas.

The doctor instructed the parents to keep the young girl at home because he thought she would die. They did everything they knew to do, such as soaking her in a tub of vinegar water, but nothing could repair the damage. Unable to put clothes on the child's badly burned body, they laid her in a crib with a sheet stretched across for a ceiling and two light bulbs for warmth. There was nothing more anyone could do for her. She was such a little girl, and she was burned so badly. Ruth longed to pick up her little girl and hold her close, but for three long weeks she had to let her lie there alone, only able to gently turn her over from time to time. Ruth prayed that God would spare her little girl's life. She knew in her heart that God had a purpose and a plan for the child's life.

The child was Jan, and day after day doctors Ivan and Nell Schultz came to the house. One day they came with a doll. Things were changing, prayers were being answered—Jan would not die, but live to fulfill God's purpose and plan for her life. That plan eventually took Jan to Northwestern College, to a church in Hersey, Wisconsin, and to the Amazon jungles of southern Colombia to share a cup of coffee and the gospel of Jesus Christ with all who came by. In that plan she would meet a young Muinane girl, Clementina, who eleven years earlier had been left to die.

Several years and thousands of miles apart, God saved two baby girls, who by human thought and reason would never make it. And what a difference those two lives have made! "Many are the plans in a man's heart, but it is the Lord's purpose that prevails" (Prov. 19:21, NIV).

Who could have guessed the plans and purposes God had for these two little girls? What similar plans might God have for the unborn, the impaired, the helpless, the despised and abused? Any one of these individuals might have become a missionary, educator, scientist, mother . . . or simply the only person who could have brought the hope of Jesus Christ to one other soul. We never know through whom the Light of the World will choose to shine most brightly.

Before Alicia walked into the jungle, God had a plan

for Clementina. Before Clementina was conceived, God spared a little girl in Iowa and purposed that she would carry the Good News deep into the Amazon jungle to a very small tribe. And as if to say, "I planned it to the very last detail," our Lord gave us one more little surprise. Clementina was born on February 28—the same day that Janice Peterson Walton was born!

You do not walk alone in your jungle. None of us does. We are all connected through the love of Christ. We must all be made whole through his blood.

CHAPTER SIX

"One of Us Is Not Too Smart, and I Have a Funny Feeling It's Me"

What have I learnt where'er I've been,
From all I've heard, from all I've seen?
What know I more that's worth the knowing?
What have I done that's worth the doing?
What have I sought that I should shun?
What duties have I left undone?
    — Pythagoras

JIM'S STORY

During our years in the Colombian jungle, the Lord saw fit to teach us many lessons. Evidently, one of his primary lessons for me was humility. And I must be a slow learner, for I was given so many opportunities to learn it.

In my youth I had done quite a bit of canoeing in the boundary waters of northern Minnesota. I could paddle a canoe in a straight line without changing the oar from side to side every few strokes. I felt at home in a canoe, and I had confidence in my abilities.

But I had learned to paddle from the back of the canoe, and the Muinane men always paddled from the front. Only the women and children paddled from the back. I watched carefully how the men drew the heart-shaped paddle through the water, pulling the front of the canoe into the desired course.

After much observation and careful study, I decided I was ready to follow the men's example. Unfortunately, I chose as my first expedition a family trip across the river to visit Chief Fernando. Jan sat in the back of the canoe, Diana and Danny in the middle, and I climbed into the front. I pushed the canoe out into the river and began to paddle. The bow of the canoe caught the current and quickly swung downstream. I managed to fight it back around, and I headed upstream toward the chief's house. But the silly canoe would not go where I told it to go, and we were again spun around to float downstream.

Diana and Danny were laughing and enjoying the wild ride. Jan didn't find the experience quite as amusing.

"Jim," she began cautiously, "why are you trying this when the children are in the canoe? It's too dangerous." I was too busy battling the current to answer, which only exasperated Jan even further.

"Jim, if you don't know how to paddle the canoe from the front, then you should be in the back."

"But all the Muinane men paddle their canoes from the front," I reminded her.

The look on her face told me what she thought of my reasoning. If pride goeth before a fall, it might also lead to an unexpected swim in the river!

I wasn't about to give up, so I tried six or eight more

times. But each attempt took us farther down the river, and I finally admitted defeat. I told everybody to turn around in their seats. The front, where I was seated, then became the back, and I paddled my family safely upstream.

Determined to do better on the way back home, and wondering what I was doing wrong, I swallowed my pride and asked the chief. He laughed as he answered, "Didn't you know that the canoe you used is missing the rudder? You can't paddle a canoe from the front without a rudder!"

My children laughing as we turned circles in the river was one thing; now the whole village knew that the white man had tried to paddle a rudderless canoe from the front. I was finding out that I wasn't so smart, not even in areas where I felt confident.

The chief was often the source of my humility lessons. After all, on my first trip to La Sabana, he had measured my house better by eye than I had with a measuring tape. But I still thought I knew a few things better than he did.

One day, while clearing a spot in the jungle to build a pigpen, I noticed that the Muinanes always seemed to toss their machetes carelessly on the ground, and the machetes were quickly covered over and lost among the leaves, vines, and branches. I, on the other hand, was careful to stick the point of my machete into the ground, with the handle up. Thus, I could quickly and easily find my machete whenever I needed it. I was not going to point out to them that it was much easier and more efficient to stick the machete into the ground. I was hoping they would notice and learn from my example.

Late in the day, the chief pulled me aside and corrected me. "Don't stick your machete into the ground like that. You always wear shoes, and if you step back against the sharp blade, you won't get cut. But we aren't wearing shoes, and if we step back into a machete that is planted in the ground and doesn't move, it will slice our foot terribly."

What is efficiency compared to injury? What are a few minutes looking for a machete worth in exchange for days or weeks of not being able to hunt, work, or even walk? I thought I would teach them a thing or two, while I was the one who needed to notice, observe, and learn.

I quickly discovered that many of my senses didn't work as well as theirs did. The Indians seem to have an almost uncanny understanding of their jungle. They recognize individual trees in the way we recognize streets and houses in the city. They have a name for every tree, animal, bird, fish, and insect, never referring to them generically as bugs or snakes, as we might do. They automatically survey the path and its surroundings, reading subtle changes in the landscape. They could examine a path and determine that a herd of 150 to 200 wild pigs had passed within the hour, including a number of sows with their young. I looked at the same path and saw a few disturbed leaves.

And the Muinanes could hear; boy, could they hear! Certainly, I heard plenty of noises in the beginning— sounds I was convinced came from a hungry jaguar or some other wild beast come to threaten my family. But they heard so much more than I did, and with much greater understanding.

Late one afternoon, when I was tired of struggling with nouns and adjectives and participles, Lorenzo came by and offered me an excuse to set aside my translation efforts for the day. He was going hunting, and he invited me, and my shotgun, to go along. I convinced myself that the lessons I could learn while hunting would be so valuable that I didn't dare miss such an important opportunity. Further work on the language would have to wait until the next day.

I followed Lorenzo into the jungle. We had walked only a short distance when Lorenzo slowed, raised his hand, and motioned for me to stop. He cocked his head to one side, listened intently, and pointed at something in the distance.

I thought the bird was much too far away to be our next meal. If we were going to get that bird, we had some walking to do. Lorenzo reached out and picked a leaf, folded it, and blew across the flat edge to reproduce a perfect bird call. Soon the large jungle bird flew into the high branches of a nearby tree. Lorenzo continued to call the bird even closer, but to no avail. He raised the gun, squeezed the trigger, and the bird fell toward the ground. But at the last minute the wounded bird was able to stretch a wing and glide far from sight.

I began to utter a sigh of disappointment, when I was quickly hushed again by Lorenzo's raised hand. We waited a few seconds in silence, then Lorenzo took off running through the dense jungle. I had difficulty keeping up with him. I tripped, fought my way around and under branches and out of vines, but I dared not lose sight of Lorenzo. I wasn't sure where we were headed, what we were after, or if something was after us. Truth-fully, my only concern was being sure I got out of the jungle and back home.

When I eventually caught up to Lorenzo, he was sit-ting on a tree trunk that stretched across a stream. Lorenzo stared down at the water as it flowed beneath the log.

I dropped down beside him to catch my breath. "So where were you going in such a hurry?"

"Here, of course," he answered. "Didn't you know we were coming here?"

Didn't I know? How was I to know? Nobody had said anything to me. He just took off running!

"Didn't you hear the bird fall into the water?" Lorenzo continued. "This little stream is the only water around. You watch: If the bird does not get tangled in the grass or branches along the edge of the stream, it will float right here to us."

"Oh, I see," I answered automatically, but I thought it was all a little ridiculous. Still, I was content to go along with his foolishness because it would let me rest awhile before he took me off through the jungle underbrush again.

Just then it appeared: the dead bird floating on the water, drifting slowly toward us, exactly as Lorenzo had predicted. As the bird floated under the log, Lorenzo leaned down and scooped it out of the water.

A Brazilian Indian once told translator Steve Sheldon, "The reason you do not see the animals in the forest is because you have very small vision. We have large vision because we see, not only with our eyes, but with our ears, our sense of smell, with our total being. You look only with your eyes and so you have only tiny, tiny vision, and you see very little."

In all of life, we must see with more than our eyes, and we must listen with more than our ears. Maybe if we listened with our eyes, with our minds, and especially with our hearts, we would spend less time lost in the jungle of misunderstandings and broken relationships. Perhaps this is partly what Christ meant when he said, "For this people's heart has become calloused; they hardly hear with their ears, and they have closed their eyes. Otherwise they might see with their eyes, hear with their ears, understand with their hearts and turn, and I would heal them" (Matt. 13:15, NIV).

If a child does not pay attention or does not obey, the Muinanes will accuse him of not having holes in his ears. Surely if he had holes in his ears, so he could hear, he would obey. I wonder how often I could have been accused of not having holes in my ears—not only in my relationships with others, but in my relationship with God. God gave us holes in our ears, the capacity to hear his voice, but he will not force us to listen and obey. Sometimes we let the noise of the world ring too loudly, unconsciously blocking out the voice of God. Other times we deliberately put our fingers in our ears as we argue that God is silent.

I imagine that I have been guilty of both charges at times. But in the jungle, I learned the difference between hearing and truly listening, between perceiving and understanding. One of these lessons came to me, oddly enough, through a gift of beans.

We were running out of food, and there was little or none available in the village. We cooked our last meal of rice the day before the plane was scheduled to pick us up and take us to Lomalinda for a brief stay. We were thankful it was the dry season and the plane would not be delayed by bad weather.

We didn't count on the plane being required for a medical emergency. The radio operator informed us that the plane would not arrive in La Sabana for three more days.

Radios are nice at times because nobody ever sees or hears your first reaction. I knew that my fellow missionaries and people around the world were listening on the radio-net, wondering what I would say and how I would react to this turn of events. So I sat and thought a minute before pushing the button on the microphone to respond. I couldn't wait too long, however, or those listening would know I was upset.

As I remember, I didn't say much. I simply answered, "I see. Well, we will see you in three days. Pray for us. We are completely out of food, and there isn't any food in the village."

We asked around for food, but there was none. Someone brought a little casabe bread, but most of them had only what they needed for their own families. There were four in our family, plus the two Muinane men helping us with the language and two men cutting firewood. We needed food for eight people, and the little bit of casabe bread was not nearly enough.

Word of our plight spread through the village, and later that day a woman came to ask if we ate beans.

"Yes!" I answered eagerly. "Do you have some?"

"Well, maybe," she answered. "At least I know where to find some, but they are not like real beans. We don't usually eat them, but they can be eaten," she assured us. "Remember though, you *must* cook them very well or they will make you sick."

I looked at Jan and we agreed. We didn't think to ask what she meant by "cook them very well." We had no other food, and we figured our pressure cooker would *really* cook them well. The bean pods were about three feet in length and the beans inside resembled huge lima beans. Jan pressure-cooked them on top of the mud stove for three hours, until they no longer looked like beans. They were just a green mush that looked like pea soup. We all began to eat the beans heartily.

The Indians were the first to be affected. Soon we all felt sick. Danny and I were able to get rid of some of the poison before it entered our system, but Jan and Diana were not as fortunate. They developed high fevers and were very sick. We all spent the next two days in bed.

The shaman heard we had eaten the beans and came to see if we were still alive. We then discovered what "cooking them well" truly meant. Manuel explained, "The beans have a very poisonous gas in them that must be cooked out. You must cook them in an open kettle for seven days, pouring the water off each day, so that they are cooked seven times. Then you can eat them."

We had thought we were cooking them well, but we had actually captured all the gas that should have been allowed to escape. Yet it did solve one of our problems: It no longer mattered that we had no food. No one felt like eating for the next three days anyway. To this day, Diana and Danny dislike lima beans because they look so much like the strange poison beans of the Amazon.

We sometimes felt that every day brought not only a new adventure but a new lesson to be learned. I was eager to learn, grow, and be stretched to greater levels of understanding. But did growth always have to be accompanied by embarrassment, sacrifice, or suffering? Well, usually.

Late one afternoon, Manuel and Cecilia stopped by for a surprise visit. In spite of our typical shortage of food, we invited them to join us for dinner. Jan prepared a delicious kettle of soup, along with a large serving of casabe bread to serve as the main filler for the meal.

We sat up to the table and, in good American style, Jan passed the large plate of casabe bread to Cecilia first. Cecilia looked a little surprised. We watched in amazement as she took one piece and then opened her carrying bag and dumped the whole plate of bread into her bag.

This was our first illustration of an important Muinane custom: Each person is given what he or she is intended to keep. Most food is eaten on the spot, but if presented with a large pineapple, fish, monkey, or any large amount of food, the person will sample a little, but knows that you intend for them to take the rest home.

Jan was counting on the casabe bread to complement the soup and to fill up our guests, and now it was gone! Generosity was a priority to Jan. She had put all the casabe bread we had on the plate, which she passed first to Cecilia. Jan quickly recovered from the shock of seeing a major part of the meal suddenly disappear. She carefully divided the remaining food into individual portions and continued serving the meal.

This custom may seem strange to Americans, but in many ways it is a logical system. Each person is given what is meant especially for him or her. If a man is given the tail of the fish, he would not complain that he should have been given the head. Life with the Muinanes somehow seemed fair—not equal, but fair. No one thought it strange or wrong of us to give an old blind woman more than the others. We might be expected to share what little powdered milk we had with a sick child who could not nurse, but we would not be expected—even though asked—to give milk to everyone.

After I grew accustomed to this practice, I remembered Christ's parable of the workers in the vineyard. The landowner promised the men a denarius for their work in his vineyard. But throughout the day he added more workers, even up until the last hour. When the latecomers received the same pay as those who worked all day, the men who were hired first became angry. They saw equity in wages but unfair treatment. In contrast, the Muinanes often see uneven distribution but never consider it unfair.

Sometimes I wonder if the rules of our egalitarian society make it more difficult for us to understand and accept the fairness of God. We tend to feel that life cannot be fair unless it is equal. But God gives each of us exactly what we need—no less, and often no more. Our share of talents, blessings, and possessions may not seem equal to our neighbor's, but God's goodness and justice cannot be measured in temporal riches. The Muinanes' concept of "fairness without equality" helped us come to a deeper understanding of the ways God works in individual believers' lives.

In hundreds of ways, the Muinanes were teaching and training us. With great patience they gave us the tools by which we could finally minister the Word of God to them in their own language and in their own culture. It was humbling at times to realize that our own lives depended on the Muinanes' knowledge of the jungle; however, that was part of God's plan and provision for us. After all, as Lord of the jungle, God knew exactly what we needed.

The Muinanes taught me much, and the Lord used them to teach me even more. I didn't simply learn about canoeing, hunting, and cooking beans. I learned about humility and grace. I learned to listen more closely to the sounds of nature and the voice of God. Mostly, I learned about my Lord, whose love is strong enough to teach a stubborn paddler who truly steers the boat.

CHAPTER SEVEN

Finding the Footprints of God

> *We shall not cease from exploration*
> *And the end of all our exploring*
> *Will be to arrive where we started*
> *And to know the place for the first time.*
> —T. S. Eliot in "Little Gidding," *Four Quartets*

JIM'S STORY

When we first went to La Sabana, we assumed we were entering a spiritual primeval forest—a land where few, if any, Christian feet had ever trod. We were going to bring the gospel to untouched souls, to bring light into a dark world. We soon realized our naivete, if not our vanity, in believing that our presence preceded God's. On those unknown jungle trails, we found the footprints of God, who had gone before us, preparing the way.

Day by day, we learned to look for God behind the small touches in the overall patterns of life—events that fit together when perhaps they might not or should not; precise timings that went beyond simple random happenings; subtle ironies that were chock-full of grace.

As you recall, I met Andrés, the oldest son of Chief Fernando, on my first day in La Sabana. He had watched me with barely disguised interest as I read from my New Testament. At that moment I was completely unaware that God had just performed several miracles of time and circumstance.

Andrés lived three days away from La Sabana with his mother, near the Caquetá River. Indebted to a rubber baron for a transistor radio, Andrés worked rubber in the jungle far from his home, and his days were filled with hard work and monotonous routine. Because the latex flows most freely in the morning, Andrés slipped out of his hammock at the first hint of dawn each day. He hurried through the jungle and made short incisions in the bark of his trees. Then he made a small cup by folding up the sides of a leaf and pinning them together with a twig. After placing this leaf cup on the ground to catch the dripping latex, he made his way several hundred yards through the thick jungle to the next of his trees. One trail would wander in serpentine fashion back and forth to each of the nearly two hundred rubber trees dotted over that hundred-acre section of jungle.

By midmorning the leaf cups were all in place at the base of the trees, catching the small white drops of latex destined for the outside world. Andrés kept a watchful eye on the sky; even the smallest rain shower would wash the precious liquid from the cups. In a jungle that gets well over three hundred inches of rain per year, such showers were a frequent frustration.

By noon Andrés was on the trail again, collecting the morning's drippings, leaf by leaf, dumping them into gal-

Our first view of
the Cahuinarí
River.

The river was
cial to the life
of our new
friends—the
Muinanes.

When the men were taken away to gather rubber, they had to leave their canoes and families for months at a time.

Had it not been for a small plane, like this one, Janice would likely have died in 1967.

Diana and Dan came to love the jungle food, such as the large fish here shared by Chief Fernando.

Clementina was left to die at birth, but the Lord had special plans for her life.

"Granny" Margarita—one of a handful of Muinanes to survive the cruelties of the rubber era.

Jan shows a new hymnbook to Alicia and her son. The people were amazed that we could sing their words.

Magdalena came to ask Jim to pull her tooth and to ask what happened when a man stepped on the moon.

Diana and Virgelina's joyous friendship deepened the day Virgelina opened her heart to Jesus.

Carrying wood for mom's stove was a normal part of Dan's day.

Building on poles let the snakes, wild pigs and jaguars walk under, rather than through, our house.

Playing side by side with the Muinanes made a lasting impression on Diana and Dan's worldview.

Jan cooked hundreds of family meals on this mud stove that Jim made.

Aurelia washes bitter manioc to remove the last of the poison in preparation for making *casabe* bread.

Jim pulls Arturo's tooth (Jim's least favorite task). Arturo later became the local dentist.

Inéz, Regina, and many others spent weeks weaving leaves for the roof of our jungle home.

Diana baby-sat Muinane children, which allowed their mothers to teach Jan the language.

Andrés's intense search for a meaning to life led him to a personal faith in Christ and a partnership in translating the Scriptures.

Jim and Chief Fernando check the accuracy of the translation with consultant Stan Schauer.

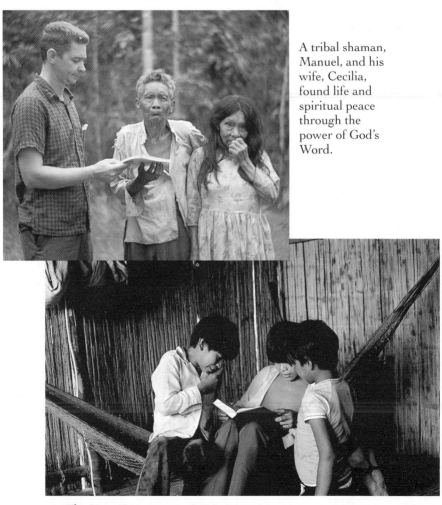

A tribal shaman, Manuel, and his wife, Cecilia, found life and spiritual peace through the power of God's Word.

The New Testament arrives!

lon canteens. He arrived back at camp late in the afternoon and then began processing the day's collections, turning the white liquid latex into sheets of congealed black rubber. This rubber sheet was then pressed between heavy metal rollers, much like running clothes through a washing machine wringer, to remove excess moisture. The rubber sheets were bundled together and later picked up when the rubber baron's launch returned.

Andrés told us the story of one particular night in the summer of 1964, while he was working rubber far from home. Hoping to relieve the monotony of the jungle, he grabbed his transistor radio and slowly moved the needle up and down the dial.

Andrés explained, "It was at a time when I was looking for answers, for meaning in life. I wanted to know where we came from, why we were alive, and where we go after we die. I had lived for almost twenty years, learning the old stories and legends from my father and grandfather. I had looked inside and outside my culture and had found no answers to my longing for truth."

The dial on his radio stopped on a strong, clear signal. The man on the radio was reading from a book: "The sun [shall] be darkened, and the moon shall not give her light, and the stars shall fall from heaven, and the powers of the heavens shall be shaken: And then shall appear the sign of the Son of man in heaven: and then shall all the tribes of the earth mourn, and they shall see the Son of man coming in the clouds of heaven with power and great glory" (Matt. 24:29-30).

That night the moon did not give light, just as the book had said, and the entire jungle was in blackness. This

strange phenomenon convinced Andrés that the book
the man read from was true, and thus might have the
answers he sought. Andrés told us, "I did not understand
much of what the man said, but I knew that the book he
read contained the truth. I had to find that book! I had to
find the truth."

A short time later the rubber baron came in his motor
launch and returned the Indians and the bundles of rubber to the Caquetá River. Andrés arrived home to hear
the news that his grandfather, in La Sabana, was dying.
Andrés walked the three days by trail to see his grandfather, reaching La Sabana one day before Stan and I
arrived on our survey trip. The very next day he heard
me read from the Bible in front of his father's guest house.

Andrés said later, "When I saw you reading that book,
I knew it was the book—the book from the radio, the
book that had the truth. And when you said it was God's
Word and you wanted to put it in my language, I determined to help you." And he did.

Andrés worked with us for more than eighteen years,
with only a few short periods when he became discouraged, disillusioned, or when family difficulties hindered
him. He became our main cotranslator, helping us translate the complete first draft of the New Testament, and
later played a major role in translating a summary of the
Old Testament.

Calling it "coincidence" would not explain all that
happened, especially since Andrés was unaware of two
key pieces of the story. First, Andrés did not know the
physical cause for the darkening of the moon that night
in the jungle. The scriptural passage seemed to perfectly

portray the unknown phenomenon that was occurring before his eyes. God surely must have planned that particular message to be broadcast at exactly the right time — because on that night, a total eclipse occurred over Andrés' part of the Colombian jungle. Perfect timing, from an all-knowing God.

Perhaps even more significant is that the story actually began at least three years earlier. In August 1961, the Lord spoke to a man named Dr. Paul Freed, president of Trans World Radio. Dr. Freed once wrote:

> When we lag behind His schedule, or try to shove out ahead of Him, the alarm is sure to go off to warn us. That is what happened that day in August when God stopped me . . . and for several reasons: among others, to teach me deep truths, and to provide a powerful means of penetrating far corners that had never been reached with His truth. (Paul E. Freed, *Towers to Eternity* [Waco, Texas: Word Books, 1968])

His vision of communicating the gospel took Dr. Freed to Puerto Rico in February 1962 to investigate the possibilities for a super-power station to carry the Good News to a larger audience. Construction on the transmitter and diesel building began in September 1963 in Bonaire, and by August 1964 the programming was in full swing. The radio message Andrés heard in June or July of 1964 must have been one of the very first broadcasts of Trans World Radio from Bonaire!

The interwoven aspects of this story never cease to amaze me. Through a radio intended to enslave Andrés, the Lord brought a message to free him. Andrés tuned to the right station at the right time. The radio minister chose the perfect passage for the greatest possible influence on Andrés' life. The Trans World Radio broadcasts began airing just in time. And Stan and I certainly arrived in La Sabana on the right day. We'll never know how life might have been different if any one of these factors had varied, but we hold steadfastly to one assurance: "In all things God works for the good of those who love him, who have been called according to his purpose" (Rom. 8:28, NIV).

As with the New Testament story of Philip and the eunuch, whenever and wherever a soul is searching for truth, God sends a messenger. Surprisingly, I occasionally found myself on the other side of the message, receiving instruction through unexpected sources.

All our lives, Jan and I had been taught that God deals directly with us in revealing his will. Many Scriptures support this—verses such as "I guide you in the way of wisdom and lead you along straight paths" (Prov. 4:11, NIV). As Christians, we had a direct line to God, didn't we?

But in the jungle, God didn't always seem to work according to our evangelical textbook! Again and again, we saw God's will and power revealed to us secondhand, through the mind and wisdom of an unregenerate, uneducated chief.

One such incident occurred while we were translating the seventh chapter of the book of Matthew.

"That's it! That's what my father told us!" Andrés exclaimed. His voice quivered with excitement, and the words would hardly come fast enough. "We must get this whole story translated and take it to the village right away!"

"Yes, of course, as soon as we—"

"My father must be told this immediately!" Andrés was emphatic. "He already knows! I tell you, Jim, my father already knows. He has told us this exact story many times!"

"Wait, slow down. Tell me again carefully," I said. "What do you mean? Did he hear it at the mission when he took the children to school?"

"No, this happened long before there was a church or mission in our jungle. Maybe fifteen or twenty years before. My father was young. He became very ill, and his spirit left him—he died." This is how the Muinanes describe a person who loses consciousness and lapses into a coma.

"His body was in this world, but his spirit left his body. His spirit walked down a trail in the jungle until that trail stopped and another appeared. The new trail was wider and clear of obstacles. It seemed to stretch straight and flat before him with no roots to trip over, no vines or underbrush to hinder him. He was about to turn down this wide, easy trail when a voice behind him said, 'Don't take that trail, it will not lead you to God!'"

Fernando never saw the one who spoke. He only heard the voice telling him to take the smaller trail that went straight ahead. At first he had not even noticed the trail because vines covered the entrance.

"It was a narrow, steep path," Andrés continued, "with roots and logs to crawl over. My father listened to the

voice and walked down the small trail. After some time
he came to an opening of light, but still could see no one.
There was only the voice that spoke from behind him,
saying, 'You are not ready to enter. You must go back to
the earth, and when you are ready, you will return here.'"

What was Andrés telling us? Did he expect us to believe
that God spoke directly to his father before the gospel was
ever known in the tribe? Such a thought challenged our
neat and tidy theology. Sure, the Old and New Testaments
are alive with visions, dreams, and signs. Such wonders
accompanied each fresh encounter by Jehovah God with a
new group of people in the Old Testament, each new revelation of Jesus, and every major outpouring of the Holy
Spirit during New Testament times. Signs, visions, and
dreams were given to substantiate the claims of Christ—
that he was the Son of God.

But we live at a time when we have the full Scriptures.
The revelation is complete, and the Word has removed
the need for accompanying signs and wonders to authen-
ticate the message or the messengers—or so we thought.
We had been taught the need for spectacular miracles
ended with the apostolic times. For us to even consider
that God would prove himself by a sign or a dream would
be like traveling backwards in time.

We were stumped. Our American Christian theology
and experiences were already on a collision course with
another culture, a different world. We had always had
the Word as long as we had lived, and we did not seek a
sign, but trusted God's Word. We were taught, "Blessed
are they that hear the word of God, and keep it" (Luke
11:28) and "It is better to trust in the Lord" (Ps. 118:8).

But the Muinanes didn't have God's commandments or his Word. They had no books, no magazines, no tracts, no newspapers—they had no writing! They had a language—a beautiful, intricate, and complex language—but until we came, it was only spoken. No one had ever produced an alphabet for the Muinanes. They did not know the God of heaven, much less his Son Jesus or the Holy Spirit. Having no Bible, they were still waiting to hear from God. How would God reveal himself to them, and how would they recognize the truth?

Our concepts of God were being sharpened by our new awareness of God's mysterious ways. God continued to overflow the edges of our mold. At times we cautiously looked around and wondered if another mold—another sector of God's church, another set of doctrines—might better explain or answer the contradictions we faced.

Serving with an interdenominational faith mission gave us many opportunities to examine and evaluate the doctrinal principles and positions of our colleagues, as well as our own beliefs. At first it was like a maze, and we wondered if any set of doctrines was right. Then we discovered, to our amazement, that each offered a special or unique contribution to understanding and approaching the one true God.

We did not change our doctrines or our faith, but Chief Fernando's dream caused us to see how we limited God by our expectations. We thought we knew how God was supposed to interact and communicate. We thought we knew the mind of God, but God proved to be much bigger than our understanding.

Fernando had this dream more than twenty years

before we arrived, and he continued to repeat it until it became the Muinanes' dream. Andrés explained, "We did not think anyone else knew our dream. We didn't know the meaning. We only knew God spoke to my father and someday God would tell us more. And he did!"

God did speak again. In a multitude of ways, some quite unusual, God continued to speak to the Muinanes and open their eyes to his truths. And he did the same with us. At first we were as surprised as Balaam must have been when he was instructed by his donkey; but we ultimately grew accustomed to hearing God's voice in the language of the Muinane. If the path you travel seems untrod and you feel alone in your journey, look closely. You will yet discover the footprints of God. And listen carefully for the voice behind you. You never know what language God will use.

CHAPTER EIGHT

No Word for Peace

This is no case for violence or hurt, since religion cannot be forced. It must be conducted by words, more effective than blows in a matter affecting the will.
—Lactantius

JIM AND JAN'S STORY

We grew up in small-town Minnesota and Wisconsin in the 1940s and 1950s, where people rarely honked their car horns. Some over-anxious teenager might bump his horn to give a small toot, but even that was considered rude. You might as well walk up to someone and say, "Hey, get out of here!" Imagine the cultural conflict when we went to live in Bogotá, where some claim that a horn is more important than brakes. Jim's dad came to visit, and while trying to cross a busy street, exclaimed, "This is truly the city of the 'quick or the dead.'"

We had even a greater conflict of a different sort when we went to live in the jungle. Where we came from, no one commanded God. Our churches taught us respect for the Almighty, and our petitions were requests, at times even a little apologetic.

The structure for the Muinane petition, on the other hand, is an imperative. Rather than requesting a certain action, you command it. If that person does not want to give, act, or do what you ask (command), he says no. If he wants to do what you request, he answers yes. If you try to ask a question, no one understands what you want, and you get no answer.

In our early weeks in the village, we would ask if the villagers had any jungle fruit or meat to sell to us. At first, they were puzzled. Then they would say, "If you command me, I will sell it to you." Well, we certainly were not going to do any such thing! What might anthropologists say about us if we made them sell us food when they had so little for themselves? We only asked them for food when they had been on a hunt or when we were sure they had extra; but to us, it would be rude to command them.

On another occasion we asked one of the villagers to accompany us to Lomalinda for a language workshop. We had discussed the possibility of going, and everyone knew how eager he was to attend. Yet each time we asked if he would be willing to go, he answered, "If you command me to go, I will go." Again, we weren't about to command him to go with us. After all, shouldn't some part of Emily Post's etiquette apply even in the jungle?

We struggled a long time in this area of language learning. Finally, we reexamined some similar cases found in our own language. For example, if your son has left the door open for the hundredth time, you might ask, "Are you going to leave the door open?" The surface structure of your conversation is a question, but there is also an underlying command. Both you and your child know that you do not intend to ask a question; what you are really saying is, "Close the door!" The Muinane system was the reverse: What seemed like a command to us was actually a question.

When we began translating the Lord's Prayer, we realized how demanding it sounds in the English language: ". . . thy kingdom *come,* thy will *be done* on earth as it is in heaven. *Give* us this day our daily bread, and *forgive* us our debts, as we forgive our debtors, and *lead us not* into temptation, but *deliver* us from the evil one. . . ." Are we commanding God when we pray this way? Of course not, for we are following Christ's example. Perhaps the Muinanes weren't so wrong after all.

We discovered many such challenges as we tried to learn the language and ultimately translate the Bible for the Muinanes. Many people believe that the language of those living in a primitive area of the world would be very simple. The Muinane language is anything but simple. For example, using the wrong tone in talking about "the Word of God" changes the phrase to mean "the yesterday of God." A difference in the length of a vowel determines whether salvation is found in a name or in a jungle fruit.

An unwritten language has no textbooks, no phrase books, no dictionary, no literature of any kind. The question was, where should we begin?

A few of the Muinanes were bilingual and could speak the national language, which is Spanish, but it was limited to their dealings with the outside world. Muinane was spoken by everyone living at La Sabana. If we were going to communicate with the Muinanes and be understood, it would have to be in their own language.

Everyone in La Sabana used the Muinane language for public and private interaction. Even the multilingual Muinanes were proud of their own language. The Muinanes were the *Miyam+naa*—the "real people," and they spoke "real" words. As we began to live in La Sabana, learn their words, and uncover the intricacies and beauty of their language, we came to agree that Muinane is one of the world's loveliest languages.

We began analyzing the Muinane phonology, its sound system. One step was to distinguish between a pair of sounds by specifying differences in articulation. We discovered that at times a difference in articulation did not signal a different letter in the alphabet, but only a different pronunciation. If this were ignored, we would be understood, but such an accent would always make us sound foreign to the Muinanes.

The Muinane language has no [th] sound, so it would be very hard for a speaker of Muinane to pronounce English words such as *the* and *this* or names such as Matthew and Timothy. We were glad that we had come to learn their language and not to teach them English.

During the eighteen years it took us to translate the New Testament for the Muinanes, we never stopped learning their language. The beginning, however, may have been the most exciting, because the distinguishing of letters, or speech segments in Muinane, was the start of creating their written alphabet—the first step in bringing literacy to them.

Beyond our personal excitement at being the first
"white people" to learn the Muinane language, we felt
that we were also helping the Muinanes by broadening
their opportunities for growth of mind and spirit. We
were also helping the nation of Colombia by opening cor-
ridors of understanding, communication, and education
to one of their minority groups. We were even serving
the international academic community by exploring and
making data available on one of the world's unwritten
languages.

Were we linguists or missionaries? Our mission was to
bring the message of salvation, the gospel of Christ, to
the Muinane people. Our methods included analyzing
their language, forming a dictionary, and translating the
Scriptures. Since we wanted to learn the language and be
able to write it down for the Muinanes, we did it in a sci-
entific way. We didn't want to have to tell the Muinanes,
when we completed the translation, "This is God's Word,
but the grammar is poor." God wanted to speak good
Muinane!

We learned, among many interesting things, that the
Muinane alphabet has six vowels—one more than the
English alphabet. At first it was hard to distinguish this
extra vowel [+] from the [u] sound. We also had some
difficulty with their additional consonant, the glottal stop.
Though we may not realize it, we make the glottal stop
sound in English every time we say "oh oh." If you say
"oh oh" slowly, you will feel a little stop, or catch, in your
throat between the first and second "oh." Because this
stop, or catch in the throat, carries no meaning in
English, we do not write it, and so many English speak-

ers are unable to hear it. This catch, or glottal stop, however, is as important to the Muinane language as the letters *p, t,* or *k.*

These subtleties in the language may seem unimpor-
tant, but it was crucial that we learn to make these dis-
tinctions. One tiny error or omission could mean the
exact opposite of what the Bible actually says. One
wrong letter in Matthew 18:5 would render the verse,
"And any of you who *casts away* a little child like this
because you are mine, is welcoming me and caring for
me." The subtleties of the Muinane language might be
likened to the nuances of our own or our parents' languages: an English accent ['], the Spanish tilde [~], or the
German umlaut [¨] can make a world of difference.

In Old Testament times, the men of Gilead used the
subtleties of language as a weapon in their war with
Ephraim (Judg. 12:6). If a fugitive attempted to escape
past the guards at the Jordan River, he was asked to say
Shibboleth. If he said *Sibboleth,* they knew he was an
Ephraimite, for the Ephraimites could not pronounce the
sound *sh.*

A very similar experience once opened a locked door
for us—literally. We were returning to Colombia from
the States during an extremely dangerous time. Due to
terrorist activity, it was not safe to communicate our time
of arrival or other travel details.

After clearing customs at Bogotá's Eldorado Airport,
we caught a cab. As we drove north, the city lights went
out and a large section of the city was in a blackout. We
arrived outside our mission guest house shortly before
midnight. The cab driver, not wanting to flirt with danger

on a dark street in Bogotá, quickly dumped our suitcases onto the street and drove off.

Jim reached through the steel security bars and knocked on the door. No answer. We nervously glanced up and down the darkened street and then knocked again. We waited, and then we thought maybe we heard something on the other side of the door. Finally we heard a soft, uncertain question: "Who's there?"

We now knew that someone was home, but getting in would not be easy. Only weeks before, someone had knocked on that same door and seven terrorists, armed with automatic weapons, burst in, tied up the occupants, and took one of the missionaries. Now the missionary was dead, the mission was still under terrorist threat, and it was nearly midnight in an area with no electrical power. The woman inside wasn't particularly eager to open the door.

We eagerly answered her question, "The Waltons. We're Jim and Jan Walton."

The answer came back in huffed disbelief, "No, you're not! Jim and Jan are in the United States."

In spite of our repeated assurances, she was not convinced. We were getting quite nervous, scanning the street for any signs of danger. How could we get inside before something happened?

The voice from inside asked, "If you're Jim Walton, what are you doing out there?"

It was no use. We might talk our way into a lot of places, but we weren't going to talk our way into that house, that night. Jim finally answered, "I'm just standing out here waiting for somebody to let me in."

The locks turned, the door opened, and we were welcomed into the group house by our colleague Johanna. "What made you open the door?" we asked after we were safely inside.

"Easy," she said. "When you answered, 'I'm just *standing* out here,' I knew you were a native English speaker. A Colombian would not have so easily pronounced the *a* in *standing* with the correct vowel quality."

Pronunciation may have saved our lives that night, but language is much more complex than stringing sounds together. When we began analyzing Muinane words, we were in for a big surprise. The Muinane language will express in one word what may take three or four words in English. Often an entire English phrase is compressed into just one Muinane word. This doesn't make Muinane more or less efficient than English, just different.

The deeper we got into the language, the more we learned and the more eager we were to translate. It was fairly easy to converse when we could control the topics and talk about the day, the weather, the things we knew. It was quite another matter when we began to translate. We couldn't skip over hard words or leave out a difficult concept. We were eager to translate the message of salvation, the gospel of peace, into Muinane. Imagine our dismay when we were told that the Muinane language had no word for "peace."

Had they never had a word for peace? Had they endured such cruelty, hardships, and suffering that they lost their word for peace? Some Muinanes suggested that we use the Spanish word *paz.* Others disagreed, because few, if any, understood the Spanish word. It would fill a word space, but it would be a word with zero meaning. That was not acceptable to us, but no one could help us find a word for "peace." We asked the old, the young, the chief, the shaman, men, women—almost everybody, nearly every day. The answer was always the same: "We have no word for this."

Every language in the world contains a wealth of nuances, shades of meaning, and the potential to express every concept, notion, and idea. Languages use different grammatical forms, words where we use phrases or phrases where we use words; but whatever they need to say, they can say. We were convinced that everything in Scripture could be said in Muinane. We just needed to find out how they would say it. We also needed to know how they wouldn't say something.

We were translating 1 Thessalonians 5:5-8, where the apostle Paul wrote that we are to be like those who walk in the light of day, our lives should contrast the life of those who sleep and are drunken in the night, and we are to be sober. We fell upon what we thought to be a convenient metaphor in Muinane: "people of the day." It was close to "children of the day," as the Scripture read, and it seemed to fit so well in the translation. Then we noticed the Muinanes use this phrase most frequently in a derogatory manner. We checked more closely regarding its meaning.

A "person of the day" was one who brags in the daytime of the jaguars he has killed and how he knows all the old stories and traditions. When night comes and it is time to hunt the jaguar, or the men gather to retell the myths and legends, this "person of the day" is nowhere to be found. He is a braggart, a hypocrite, one who claims to be what he isn't. Needless to say, we quickly changed the metaphor in 1 Thessalonians.

In Muinane, every participant or person, when first introduced, is referred to by noun or name. In translating the Gospel of John, it was not a matter of personal preference or of whether we wanted to make it clear that "the Word" in the first verse was Christ. The language structure demanded it. If the passage was to be understood, every participant or person, when first introduced, must be referred to by noun or name. Thus, in Muinane, John 1:1 reads, "At the very first, before anything else had come to be, there was the Word of God. And this one, Christ, was with God. And he too was God."

Ambiguity seldom occurs in Muinane. By making ambiguities clear, were we doing a kind of amplification of the text? No. Everything in the source text, and only what is in the source text, is brought out in a translation. The Scripture text dictates what is translated. The target language allows some things to be explicit and others to remain implicit. Fidelity of translation requires that the meaning and the message of every word, of every jot and tittle, must be there. Nothing added, nothing left out. We applied to our work on the whole New Testament the warning of John in Revelation. "I warn everyone who hears the words of the prophecy of this book: If anyone adds anything to them, God will add to him the plagues described in this book. And if anyone takes words away from this book of prophecy, God will take away from him his share in the tree of life and in the holy city, which are described in this book" (Rev. 22:18-19,NIV).

We never felt that it was our responsibility, or our privilege, to *interpret* in the translation. What is present but implicit in the original can be explicit and clear in the translation. What is ambiguous in the original, we did not attempt to interpret and clarify. We might wish to clarify some of the more difficult passages, which, because of misinterpretation, cause confusion between churches and Christians. But we did not consider it proper, as translators, to doctor the original. We were translating God's Word, and we were to translate only what was there. The Muinanes will find their interpretation of these difficult passages—just as we must—by comparing with the rest of Scripture.

Still, in spite of all our learning and our efforts, we struggled to find a word for peace. A year went by. We asked and searched and prayed. Two years went by. Three years. Still no word for peace. Then a very difficult thing happened, an event that almost ended our work with the Muinanes.

Chief Fernando was preparing to journey to a town called Araracuara. It would take the chief three tortuous days of walking over harsh jungle trails to arrive at his destination. Araracuara was the site of a large national penitentiary and an airstrip hewn out of rock. Our mission plane would be flying to that area in a couple of days, and there would be room for Fernando on the flight to Araracuara. The chief was thrilled at the prospect of avoiding a three-day walk and even more excited about the promise of an airplane ride.

"But I must arrive on Friday," Chief Fernando reminded us.

"No problem!" we assured him. "The plane will come

99

on Thursday, a whole day before you have to be at Araracuara."

Thursday arrived and all the Muinanes came to see their chief climb inside the "flying canoe." Today would be special. Instead of three days, it would take Chief Fernando just twenty minutes to get to Araracuara. We talked and visited about the canoe that flies in the sky and how quickly it could travel. We waited for word when the plane would arrive.

Soon the radio crackled, and the pilot informed us that the weather was bad where he was, and the plane would not be coming to La Sabana. This was not good news, and the chief was not a "happy camper." He had waited for the plane and would now arrive at his destination two days late. He mumbled to his wife, hastily put together three days' provisions, and started walking. Less than an hour later, the radio crackled again. The weather was improving, and the plane would be stopping at La Sabana after all.

We sent someone running to the chief's house with the news. Chief Fernando had already left and was far down the trail, but his wife thought she might be able to catch up with him. The plane arrived, but the chief had set out walking at a phenomenal pace, and it took a fast-running Alicia longer than expected to catch up to him.

Meanwhile, we waited at the airstrip, not knowing if Alicia was able to overtake Fernando or not. Noon passed, another hour — still no word of the chief. Another hour, then the pilot said, "I can't wait any longer. If they haven't returned in fifteen minutes, I will have to leave. I need three hours flying time over the jungle to get back to Lomalinda. Sunset is at 6:21."

The engine roared as the small plane raced down the grassy airstrip, then jumped into the air. As you might have guessed, in just a short time the chief came out of the jungle, across the airstrip, and up the steps to our house. We were disappointed that the plane had left, but the chief was furious!

"Where did the plane go? Why did it leave me again? I came these many hours back, and now I will have to start all over again in the morning!"

We couldn't blame him for being upset and angry, yet we couldn't change the unfortunate circumstances. The chief was so angry that confronting us was not enough— he insisted on talking to the radio and to the tape recorder. He knew that the tape recorder heard and remembered everything he said, and it gave him a sense of being listened to.

We tried to listen, but he was talking so fast. He was using words and phrases in Muinane we had never heard before—probably some that we would never use in translating the Scriptures! We probably answered only half of his questions, as we understood only half of what he was saying. But we did hear and understand quite clearly that, as chief of the Muinanes and La Sabana and as owner of the land and the airstrip, he would never again permit the airplane to land at La Sabana. He repeated that information a number of times throughout the afternoon. It is difficult to describe how angry the chief was, but suffice it to say, we weren't altogether sure we would ever leave La Sabana—and if we did, if we would ever be allowed back in the village.

The tape recorder went on listening long after our

brains crashed from information overload. The chief
returned to his house for the night and left the next day
for Araracuara by trail.

The chief eventually recovered from his great disappointment and, in succeeding years, rode in the plane
many times. We knew the tape would provide us a lot of
new language data, so with Andrés' help, we started
translating the tape.

Throughout the tape, the chief kept saying, "I don't
have one heart." We asked, if the negative were trans-
formed to a positive, could a person have one heart with
another person? The answer was yes. "Having one heart"
would mean that there is nothing between you and the
other person. He does not owe you, and you do not owe
him. There is agreement, and everything is right between
you. There is freedom; there is nothing to hinder your
fellowship. You are no longer at war, no longer fighting.
All hostility is gone. There is no more fear.

It wasn't a word; it was a metaphor, a phrase. But it
sounded a lot like peace to us!

We had to be sure of one more factor. A person could
be at peace with another person, but would they use this
same phrase for being at peace with God? The Muinanes
said it was proper to use the phrase in relation to God,
but the idea that all of a person's debts could be canceled,
and that everything could be all right between them and
God was a strange concept. A person would no longer
need to fear God. They could have unhindered fellowship, and be at "one heart" with God. It was an amazing
concept to the Muinanes, and one that changed many
lives.

After three years and a nearly disastrous falling out with the chief, we finally had our word for peace. And it was far richer, both for the Muinanes and for us, than we could ever have imagined.

Each verse we translated revealed another aspect of God's character and opened the Muinanes' hearts and minds to the love of God. John 1:18 told them, "Nobody has seen God, only the Son who is in the Father; he is causing us to know the Father." God was being revealed to them through his Son Jesus Christ, and through the Word as it was being translated. "And the one who does not love another, does not yet know God, the God whose character it is to always love others" (1 John 4:8, Muinane). The apostle Peter encouraged his readers that they could place all their cares "into God's hand, for he is concerned for our good" (1 Pet. 5:7, Muinane).

Many other language groups in the world are still waiting to read and understand the Scriptures. Today, there are more than 300 million people who do not yet have God's Word written in their language. To them, his words are nonexistent, just black marks on a page. When the Bible is translated, it speaks to people in the language they understand deep within their hearts. It speaks of faith, hope, and love. God is telling them, "I speak your language. I love you. I sent my Son, Jesus, to die for you."

In their own language, the Muinanes could understand these concepts. They could even understand peace: having one heart with God. God was bringing peace to the Muinanes in his time, in his way; and they were able to embrace it when it arrived in their language.

Perhaps, deep inside our hearts, each of us speaks a different language. We are unique individuals, and our backgrounds, experiences, and emotions all influence the way we communicate. Certain words have different connotations and evoke different emotions for each of us. Perhaps some of our communication problems are actually translation problems, a language barrier.

Thankfully, God is multilingual. He has no communication problems. God can speak in the language of every heart.

CHAPTER NINE

Some through the Fire

Man's inhumanity to man makes countless
thousands mourn.
　　　—Robert Burns

JAN'S STORY

"I wonder how Granny is?"

Every time we flew back into La Sabana after our visits to Lomalinda or the States, our first thoughts were of Margarita, the woman everyone called Granny. Margarita was in her late seventies when we first met her and already partially blind. She was one of our special friends.

Granny came to visit as often as she could, always bringing us a gift of casabe bread. She would walk an hour and a half through the jungle, across streams on the single log "bridges." At the river, if she could not find a canoe, she would remove her clothing, wrap her gift of bread in it, and swim the swift river, holding the bread above her head to keep it dry. She would spend a few hours and then return home over the same jungle trail and across the same river—the river that some say God forgot.

Granny came to talk with the only foreigners who had ever learned her language. She spoke of happy things: her nieces and nephews, already grown and now grand-parents themselves. Though she had married three times, Margarita had no children; the jungle and its diseases had taken each husband from her. She spoke of our friend-ship and our kindness to her—though we felt it was only a brook compared to the raging river of hatred she had known in her life.

We treated her illnesses and brought her small items she needed: pieces of cloth, a few matches, some fish hooks. She was a proud woman who carefully guarded her dignity, so we let her pay us a little for these items. When she had no money—for some found it easy to steal from an old blind woman—we looked for a small job she could do or bought a piece of fruit from her.

One spring I was awaiting ear surgery and could not go to the tribe with Jim. I sent along a knife that Granny had asked for. I told Jim to give it to Granny as my gift since I would not be able to come visit her for a while. When Jim gave her the knife, she held it tight against her heart, giggled, and said, "Janice is so nice. She is the best granddaughter in the world. Tell her it is good she loves me."

Granny was right—it was good that I loved her, and I gained so much in return. A few days later, Granny brought Jim a skinny little rooster—all she had in the world. She said she wanted to send the money to me for the knife, but we knew the real reason for the gift. Granny knew Jim had no meat to eat, and she was tak-ing care of her "family."

Many in the tribe spoke of the injustices, the atrocities, and the savage brutality of the rubber barons, but Margarita was one of the few who had lived through those days of anguish and pain. She had experienced the cruelties firsthand: She endured the rubber exploitation and the massacre of her family, relatives, and tribe. Her life had been made miserable by the world's hunger for rubber.

Many years before scientists discovered the benefits of the rubber tree, the Indians had used rubber as a waterproofing material to patch their canoes. As early as 1495, Columbus reported that the natives of Haiti were observed playing with "elasticlike balls." In 1745, Charles Marie de La Condamine reported to the Parisian Academy of Science on the strange uses to which Ecuador's Indians put the white sticky sap of a tree they called *cahuchu*. It was not until 1770 that the English chemist Joseph Priestly gave it the name rubber when he found it could rub out pencil marks.

Yet for decades rubber remained little more than a novelty. Then, in 1823, a Glasgow chemist named Charles Macintosh discovered how to convert rubber into a pliable coating for fabric. It was then used to manufacture fire hoses, rain capes, overshoes, hats, and syringes. Still rubber was considered to have only slight commercial value.

That idea changed in 1842 with the discovery of the vulcanization process, which overcame the problem of rubber products becoming brittle in the winter and soft in the summer. Rubber became an important industrial raw material and an important commodity in international trade. The entire modern world was soon clamoring for rubber, and in large quantities.

In a single year, 1906, an estimated 24.5 million U.S. dollars of rubber was ferried down the upper tributaries of the Amazon to Manaus. A 20 percent tax levied on exported rubber added nearly 3 million dollars a year to the state's treasury. What had been a profitable industry now became a highly lucrative one. Even Andrew Carnegie was said to have lamented, "I ought to have chosen rubber rather than steel."

Richard Collier tells much of the story in his book, *The River That God Forgot*. This tragically true story, stranger than fiction, "took place during the early years of this century at a time when two-thirds of the entire world's rubber came from Manaus and when each ton of latex exported cost seven native lives."

Manaus, capital of the jungle state of Amazonas, was called "the pearl of the Amazon." Collier described Manaus at its height as "a city more swinging than London, more opulent than Paris, more violent than the Barbary Coast." While major U.S. cities like Boston and San Francisco used horse-drawn trams, Manaus, in the heart of Brazil's Amazon jungle, boasted one of the most up-to-date electric streetcar systems in the world, a system sponsored by the head of a U.S. rubber company. It became the first large Brazilian city to introduce electric streetlights, a full decade before Rio de Janeiro, and only seventeen years after the first workable incandescent lightbulb was created by Thomas Edison.

Manaus boasted a two-million-dollar opera house, built with iron brought from Glasgow and tiles from Alsace-Lorraine. While visiting the opera hall almost ninety-five years later, Jim was struck by the extravagance still evident in the halls covered with rich golden draperies, the stately white-and-pink marble pillars, the elegant vases of Sevres porcelain, and the paintings by Europe's finest masters.

As raw rubber flowed from the Amazon to the world's nations, the world's trade came back up the river: butter from Denmark, pasta from Milan, sauerkraut from Germany, and sweet-smelling eucalyptus from Australia. Jewels were ordered from Cartier's of Paris, and homes were filled with English furniture of the finest woods, shipped five thousand miles from London. Amazonia held the monopoly of the world's raw rubber supply and enjoyed the luxury it could buy.

The rapid rise in the demand for rubber in Europe and North America was reflected in the lush lifestyle and material abundance of Manaus. Yet all the riches, luxury, sophistication, and extravagance were only a facade. One scholar writes:

> Only if the Indians shed their own blood, as they shed the juice of the rubber tree, could gigantic dividends be made in this remote part of Amazonia that was too distant for conventional returns. For dividends to be given, a systematic slaughter was necessary. . . .
>
> These fortune hunters had come as slave masters, lords of the jungle, owners of the Indians. They ruled with force and cruelty. They beat and imprisoned those who could no longer work. They left broken bones unattended and left the sick to die. They became judge, jury, and executioner. These horrors

could only have occurred in the far corners of Amazonia, thousands of miles from civilization and from the eyes of anyone who possessed the power to stop the cruelty. In their rage to satisfy their greed, they killed whatever and whomever was necessary, wiping out entire tribes. This was not the end of a species of bird, not the destruction of a plant species, but the destruction of whole cultures. (Lucien Bodard, *Massacre on the Amazon* [London: Tom Stacey Ltd.], 1971)

The fires of hell blazed beneath this boiling cauldron of hatred, cruelty, torture, and death. For those who resisted, punishment was severe: limbs severed, eyes pierced, eyelids sewn shut, hot oil and wax poured in men's ears. Mothers, daughters, and little sisters were raped and ravaged by these savages from the civilized world. The Muinanes tell of the rubber lord's games, one of which was to soak a burlap sack in kerosene and tie it over an Indian's head. After turning him in circles and lighting the sack on fire, they would make bets as to whether he would find his way to the river or run off another direction into the jungle to die.

Crimes that would appall the most sinister of men were perpetrated on the inhabitants of La Chorrera, El Encanto, Ultimo Retiro, La Reserva, and points as remote as La Sabana, home of the Muinanes—and home of a young Indian girl named Margarita.

One day stands out in Margarita's mind, though it was probably like any other day to the fortune hunters. One of the Muinanes had been beaten and placed in stocks as a punishment for not bringing in enough rubber. Punishment was commonplace, but it was often far worse than what this man was enduring. Some were stripped and staked spread-eagle on ant hills. Others were beaten and left to die from exposure to the tropical sun, bloodsucking gnats, vampire bats, and any other animals that might wander by. Still others were hung by their feet and used for target practice.

The man in stocks was well aware of such torture—he had undoubtedly witnessed it many times—and was fearful for his life. When the rubber barons came to him with a question, he thought he had devised a plan for his escape.

The repeated beat of drums echoed through the jungle, announcing that the fruit of the *chonta* palm was ripe; the Indians were gathering for a festive harvest dance. The fortune hunters, however, had no way of knowing this, for only the Muinanes knew the message of the drums. The imprisoned Indian seized the opportunity. "The drums are speaking evil," he told his captors. "Unless you release me, they will come with their spears, clubs, and poison darts to kill you."

The men must have believed him, for they immediately gathered their guns and cans of kerosene, and set out for battle. The unsuspecting Indians saw the rubber barons approaching and thought they were coming to join in the festivities. The Indians greeted them in front of the maloka and offered their uninvited visitors small bowls of unfermented palm wine—a gesture of welcome and hospitality. But those who welcomed the visitors were shot, and the large communal house was doused with kerosene and set ablaze.

Margarita, then a teenage girl, was terrified as flaming poles and leaves began to fall on the nearly 150 Indians huddled inside. Suddenly her aunt grabbed her and thrust her through the flaming leaf wall, across the open patio, and toward the steep river embankment. Emerging figures, silhouetted by the burning flames, were easy targets for the men's rifles. All who tried to escape were killed—except the young Margarita and one other girl.

The cries of those trying to escape the blazing inferno and the crack of the rifles screamed in Margarita's ears as she plummeted down the riverbank and into the water. For a few moments all was silent as she ducked her head and swam underwater. Each time she surfaced to breathe, the terrifying sounds of death awaited her. Again and again she plunged under water and swam, until the horrifying sounds of the nightmare behind her finally died away in the distance. Still she swam on until she was exhausted, then clawed her way up the riverbank and began running deep into the forest. She ran until she could no longer run, until all she could hear were owls, crickets, and frogs—the familiar sounds of the jungle.

But her sense of safety was short lived. Young Margarita was soon hunted down and made to walk days and weeks through the jungle to a place far from the only home she had ever known, where she would spend many years in virtual slavery. More than a hundred men, women, and children—many of them Granny's family— had perished from the flames and the bullets that day.

The atrocities were so horrible, the bloodshed so great, that eventually the world could no longer tolerate the horror nor permit the insanity to continue. A young American engineer named Walter Hardenburg was taken prisoner, and it took the whole might of the U.S. State Department to secure his release. His reports shocked the world. The British government also began an investigation into the brutal slayings in the Putumayo region of South America.

Eventually the truth became known. The young American engineer taken hostage unearthed the shocking truth of what he saw taking place under rubber baron Julio Arana's rule. He dedicated his life to exposing the horrors and ending the power of Arana's rubber empire. Sir Roger Casement, engaged by the British government to shed light on the atrocities, released an exposé declaring that the forests were "battlefields of bones." The Indian population, in five years, had fallen from fifty thousand to no more than eight thousand (Collier, p. 214). In July 1912, Casement's report was published, provoking international indignation. The British House of Commons appointed an official committee of inquiry on the Putumayo affair.

Julio Arana knew his whole empire was at stake, so in March, 1913, he sailed for England to defend himself. Arana was confident that once he appeared in person, no high court judge or parliamentary commission would accuse him. Who could fail to see that he was not an illiterate commoner, but a man of influence and power? He was also keenly aware that the British Parliament could place no other punishment on him than reprimand or censure.

Despite the favorable impressions he elicited as a "gentleman, a master man, a born parliamentarian," the final committee report to the House of Commons declared: "Señor Arana, together with other partners . . . had knowledge of and was responsible for the atrocities perpetrated by his agents and employees in the Putumayo" (Collier, pp. 251, 276).

The stage was set to bring an end to the slaughter. Lucien Bodard writes, "It revealed atrocities more horrifying than the most perverted imagination could have invented, sadism's dreams. Yet it was the truth. At least 40,000 Indians liquidated, one after another."

But the terror eventually ended, not for humanitarian but for monetary reasons. Deciding it was no longer feasible to depend indefinitely on wild rubber from the tropical forests of Amazonia, businessmen had years earlier conceived a plan to smuggle the treasured rubber-tree seeds out of the heart of Amazonia's jungle and into Malaysia. On August 12, 1876, the seedlings had sailed for Colombo, Sri Lanka, and the Paradeniya Botanical Garden. Though the end of South America's cruel rubber empires would not be realized until 1913, the seeds of destruction had been planted. Amazonia's rubber boom would not die by an army, by disease, or by an act of mercy and justice, but by the plummeting price of raw rubber on the stock market.

As a teenager, Margarita escaped the fire and the bullets, then was hunted down and taken far from her home of La Sabana: Yet she had survived. Strange as it may seem to the world, God had not forgotten the river. God had not forgotten the people; God had not forgotten Margarita; God had not forgotten the suffering.

During the years of Margarita's exile, investigations started by Britain's government were completed and verdicts were rendered; rubber seeds grew on plantations in Malaysia, empires crumbled, and finally, Margarita was allowed to return home. But there was no home to return to, no family to welcome her. Only a few of her tribespeople from other malokas remained. They had also fled into the jungle, living like animals, in search of safety. The small clearing known as La Sabana was the only home that remained.

Granny didn't like to talk about those memories. When she did, her eyes, which could discern only light and shadows, would fill with tears, her voice would break, and she would sit for long periods of silence—and I would hold her hand.

For twelve years, our first question when we arrived back in La Sabana was, "How is Granny?" This time would be no different. I was eager to land and see how she was doing. She had seemed so frail when we left.

As we flew over the jungle, I thought about the cruelties she had witnessed, the atrocities she had survived. I wondered about the men who could commit such acts, seemingly without a shred of conscience or compassion. I don't understand the injustices of a world twisted by sin. I can't comprehend how greed and materialism will cause some people to exchange their ethics, virtues, and seat at God's table for life's bowl of pottage.

I know that God sees every evil and every atrocity of man; not even the jungle can hide the wrongs. God is aware and is keeping a record, a record that will be read at the appointed time. But why the Muinanes? Why sweet Granny?

And why Carl Mortensen—our friend and the designer of the new missionary plane we were traveling in? My eyes looked on Carl, so confident in the pilot's seat. He, like Granny, had reason to question God about the events of his life.

Early in his missionary career, Carl was stricken with polio and sent back to the United States. For the rest of his life, every breath was accompanied by an audible wheeze as his lungs fought for air. From a hospital bed in Lima, Peru, Mortenson began to dream of a sturdy, safe, twin-engine missionary airplane. From his dreams came the somewhat boxy but sturdy, Short Take-Off and Landing, twin-engine *Evangel*. This plane, and the subsequent *Angel* airplane, changed missions as we knew it. The efforts of one person can ultimately help the gospel reach hundreds of thousands of souls.

Carl possesses the kind of persistent faith found mostly in books, but seldom in life. Many people can dream great dreams, only to give up when they are weary and worn down by time. The people who succeed are those who have found an in-between faith. In between the dream and the victory are the battles, the hardships, the testing of one's faith. Many people, in the end, will flock to celebrate the victory. But in-between, it takes a special kind of faith to go on, and on, and on in the face of every obstacle, defying every doubt and doubter. Many of us have a starting kind of faith and are willing to attempt great things for God. Most of us have a victory kind of faith and will throw our weight behind a worthy cause or a new awakening. But all of us need the kind of in-between faith that stretches from start to finish.

Carl had this kind of faith. In a strange way, so did Granny. As a young girl, Margarita had never heard of Jehovah God. Her faith wasn't in God's mercy or kindness. I don't know how she did it, but she possessed a strength of character and a will to live that fought against insurmountable odds. And she had a kindness of heart that allowed her to love a family of outsiders, in spite of what outsiders had done to her world.

Both Carl and Granny remind me of the old song whose words proclaim:

> *Some through the waters, some through the flood,*
> *Some through the fire, but all through the blood.*
> *Some through great sorrow, but God gives a song*
> *in the night season and all the day long.*

They have walked through the flood and through the fire, just as many of us have, and God walked beside them. They have heard a song in the night; they—and we—have discovered hope in the land that God is said to have forgotten.

As soon as the *Evangel* landed and came to a stop, we unwedged ourselves from around the cargo and hurried to greet the Indians who had gathered on the edge of the airstrip. My eyes immediately darted from face to face, looking for Granny. Then I looked down the trail, for her steps were not as quick as those who had run to meet the plane. I looked for the tottering figure, probing with a shoeless foot extended before her to feel the way the path goes and avoid the obstacles in the way.

We greeted the others, including the woman who would

117

have died from snakebite except for an injection we gave her and a young boy who might have died as a child had Jim not stubbornly defied his fears of the jungle at night and walked through it to where the boy lay limp in his grandmother's arms. There were others, young and old, each claiming a memory, each one important.

But Granny wouldn't be coming. My eyes again darted toward the trail, then quickly turned away, for she wouldn't be walking that path ever again. She wouldn't come, as before, and stand staring at the ground waiting for us to say, *"Tyago, ∂iicahi?"* ("Granny, are you here?") I would never again see her toothless smile, feel her arms around me, or hear her say, "My children, you are back. Welcome home." Granny had gone to meet her Lord.

At her death, Margarita owned only a scrawny chicken or two, a string hammock, a knife, and *faith*. She knew we had come to put God's Book into her language and though she would never read, she wanted to know what the Book said. One day, by faith, she put her hand into the Savior's, and a blind Indian woman saw the print of the nails. While we were away from the village that time, Granny walked her final trail. I don't picture her stumbling or feeling for the trail with her foot, but being led by a hand she recognized by its scars.

If you get to heaven before us, look for an Indian woman who doesn't have any children around her and call, "Tyago." And when she looks up, tell her the Waltons are coming.

Yes, Granny will welcome us home one more time!

CHAPTER TEN

We Want to Go Home

It is faith's work to claim and challenge loving-kindness out of all the roughest strokes of God.
—S. Rutherford

JAN'S STORY

Some people imagine the life of a missionary to be filled with the excitement of new adventures, the thrill of discovery, the wonder of God's miraculous workings, and the joy of leading people to Christ. All of these are true.

But the missionary life is also filled with frustration at the primitive conditions, threat of unknown illnesses, loneliness of isolation and sacrifice, and sorrow for people who cannot accept the love of Christ.

Some days felt like the first scenario. On other days, all I saw was the second. We knew La Sabana was exactly where God wanted us to be, but many times during those eighteen years, we had to remind ourselves of that fact. Even when we know we are in God's will, serving him is not always easy.

One of the not-so-easy times came while Jim was away

on a survey trip to another village with fellow missionary Reggie McClendon. I had been exceptionally anxious to return to La Sabana, as we had spent a longer time than usual away from the village. A low-grade fever and other complications had put me in a hospital in Bogotá. Deciding it was most probably a strain of malaria, the doctors took blood samples and started me immediately on strong antimalarial medication. The blood samples were lost, but the doctors decided it best to continue the antimalarial treatment. When we arrived in the village, I still had two more days' worth of malaria treatment to take.

Jim left immediately with Reggie to begin the Andoque survey. Reggie's wife, LaVerne, and their three daughters stayed with me and our children in La Sabana.

Shortly after Jim and Reggie left, a family brought their small five-year-old boy, José, who was very ill. They wanted me to treat him, but there was little I could do. He ate and drank for me, but I felt that he was dying.

At the end of the day, the family took him back home and smeared his body with a black paint derived from the leaves of the Genipap tree. The Muinanes believe this will make the sick person's body displeasing to the evil spirit that has entered, causing the spirit to leave the person's body and restore healing.

I wondered, if the boy died, would they blame Jim for not being here, or blame me for the treatment? If he got better, would they credit our medicine, or the black paint and chants of the shaman? My journal records the end of my thoughts that day: "The Lord will do as he sees fit."

Three times during the evening, the Muinanes chanted over José. At 9:30 P.M. a teenage boy came and asked to borrow Jim's saw and hand plane to build a box. He said José had died. I tossed and turned most of the night, thinking of this young child and his grieving parents. I wished I could have done more, but he had been too ill. I wasn't even sure what was wrong with him, although the Muinanes undoubtedly believed the illness came from an evil curse.

When sickness strikes, the Muinanes immediately look for the cause. It is taken for granted that, whatever the symptoms, some kind of spiritual force is causing the illness. The person may have inadvertently wronged a nature spirit, causing the angry spirit to make the person ill. Or the disease might be from a foreign object sent into the victim by an evil shaman.

To discover the spiritual origin of a disease, the Muinanes employ divination by trance. They use a drug called *yaje* to induce the trance and make contact with the supernatural. Among the Muinanes, only adult males may partake of this narcotic. An assistant is present to administer an emetic, which terminates the trance.

The vision that results from the yaje-induced trance is always exactly the same for the Muinanes. The sorcerer, who has taken the drug, departs the "real world" and travels to a point above the earth. From this point, he sees the earth as a round ball, which is in direct contrast to the Muinane worldview; until very recently, the Muinanes believed the world was flat. The sorcerer travels around the world and sees many different kinds and colors of people: white, black, brown, yellow. "These people," they say, "have never been seen in our world. They only exist in the shaman's dream world." The Muinane sorcerer searches out the evil shaman that has brought the curse on the sick person. The guilty shaman can be easily picked out from the rest of the world's people, as he is seen squatting and blowing into cupped hands. The assistant allows two hours for the sorcerer to identify the evil shaman, then administers a liquid emetic. This emetic causes the person to vomit the narcotic, and he returns to a conscious state.

Therapy then consists of massaging the patient's body in such a way as to "collect the evil" into one place. The evil is then supposedly extracted by sucking, blowing, biting, or flogging with nettles. The sorcerer invokes the spirits, asking them to return the evil to the shaman iden- tified in the narcotic-induced trance. The sick person may or may not get well, but it is expected that the curse will return to the evil shaman, and that he will die from the same illness.

Early the next morning, everyone came to our house. Alicia was carrying José on her shoulder, wrapped in grave clothes. The men were digging the grave, and the women waited at our house until it was ready. Then they would bury him.

Suddenly I gasped. The boy had moved! I went closer and discovered that José was breathing.

"He's still alive!" I protested. "You can't bury him alive!" I convinced them to lay him on a small mattress placed on Jim's desk. I offered the dying boy a drink. He swallowed reflexively but remained unconscious. After talking via the radio with a nurse, I gave him a shot of vitamin B-complex, and I prayed. José died shortly after noon.

In the next days, I began to sense an extreme tiredness. The nerves in my entire body seemed as though they were exposed, and my heart thumped strangely. I felt faint and nervous the rest of the day. I thought it must be fatigue and the stress of José's death. I didn't sleep all night.

In the morning, LaVerne McClendon called our Lomalinda center via radio and talked again to the nurse. When the nurse found out what medication the doctors had placed me on, she became concerned. It was later discovered that I should not have been allowed to leave the city. This particular medication is very strong and requires frequent blood tests. We should have been discouraged from returning to the jungle while I was taking this medicine.

I felt some better, but I still had a fever and felt very weak. My feet and hands were cold, and it seemed as if my blood was not circulating well. The worst symptom was the feeling that a million ants were endlessly racing through my veins. I felt more hopeful when Jim arrived back at La Sabana, but by that night I was worse. I was unsure if this was caused by the strong malarial treatment or delayed shock from José's death.

The Muinanes, of course, had their own explanations for my illness. "You touched a dying boy. You shouldn't have done that, Jan," they reprimanded me. "Now you, too, will die. Even the whippoorwill has announced impending death."

I told them I didn't believe in such omens. I tried to be strong in my faith as an example to them. But still I got worse. After five sleepless days and nights, I continued having spasms in my stomach and chest. We finally sent for transportation, and we all flew out of the village.

The journey to Bogotá was arduous, but we finally made it and I eventually recovered and returned to La Sabana. My illness had been frightening, especially with our Muinane friends offering their views of my impending death, but it did not truly threaten my resolve to serve the Lord in Colombia. It was when my children were ill or in danger that I had my doubts and fears.

When Danny was eight years old, he became sick — very sick. His temperature registered 106 degrees. We were at Lomalinda, and the doctor there worked quickly to bring the fever down and to find the cause. We were told to put him in a tub of water and place ice packs on his wrists and ankles, where the blood flows close to the skin's surface. We were warned that we could not let the fever go that high again.

I stayed beside Danny's bed hour after hour. It seemed as if every refrigerator in Lomalinda was making trays of ice cubes, and the ice packs were applied around the clock. Friends, and even short-term visitors, volunteered to sit up through the night and help keep his body cool. I was grateful for their help, but I couldn't stand to be away from my little boy. I think I learned what it means to "pray without ceasing," for I petitioned heaven frequently and loudly. I reminded God that he had brought us here — as if he needed a reminder — and that he had promised to be with us. I guess God reminded me — and I did need the reminder — that he was with me, right there at Danny's bedside.

When the fever subsided a bit and the weather cleared

enough, we flew over the mountains to a clinic in Bogotá. The blood tests showed hepatitis. Even with a very high bile count, Danny had not immediately turned yellow as expected, which sometimes happens with children. He received the necessary medicine and was soon on his way to recovery.

When struggles came, we could go on as long as we clung to the sure hope that the One who called us would never leave us nor forsake us. We could make it as long as we knew that God would never walk away from us. He never did.

In the summer of 1974, when Diana was fourteen years old, we had another medical emergency. Diana contracted a severe eye infection. We had seen this type of infection before and knew there was only one antibiotic to which it would respond. Without electricity and refrigeration, we were unable to keep a supply of medicines in the jungle, and we didn't have the needed antibiotic ointment. We tried the solutions and drops we had on hand, but the infection became worse.

By the time the medication was flown in, Diana's eye was swollen shut, and Jim needed help to pry it open in order to put the medication into her eye. I couldn't bear to look, and I turned aside. Tears rolled down my cheeks as Diana cried from the pain. I cried from fear that she might lose her sight, and from guilt for bringing her into the jungle, so far from medical assistance. I also cried as I saw the tears streaming down Jim's face, his father-heart broken because he couldn't protect his little girl from all pain and harm.

Was it the tears, the medication, or the prayers that

brought physical healing to Diana's eye and restored vision? I believe God heals in many ways. He may choose to heal through a doctor, through modern or traditional medicine, through our bodies' own restorative powers, or through a miracle. I do not prefer one above the other; I believe them all to be effective tools for God's healing.

My real spiritual struggle comes with the question, *Could I have been content if God had chosen not to heal?* I'm still not absolutely certain I know the answer to that question. The apostle Paul wrote, "I take pleasure in infirmities, in reproaches, in necessities, in persecutions, in distresses for Christ's sake: for when I am weak, then am I strong" (2 Cor. 12:10). But these were my beloved children. If answering God's call to the jungle had ultimately resulted in their deaths, would I have considered the cost of obedience too high? My only answer lies in another question: Did Christ?

JIM'S STORY

God was always with us in the jungle. He was never absent, never too busy, never late. I see this so clearly in retrospect; I wish I could have always been as sure at the time. Sometimes, in the midst of the battle, in the pain of the moment, in the dark of night, we forget what we know to be true. One day on a jungle airstrip, I forgot, and I called out to God to send me home.

I had tried the mission field and found it difficult. It demanded selflessness and sacrifice. I wasn't sure I wanted to continue. I was tired of the loneliness, the weariness, the pain, the demands, the discouragement, the opposition. There were too few rewards. I was weary from the uphill struggle of trying to win the Muinanes to Christ. At times I wondered why we ever set sail for the mission field. We could have remained in a familiar place, where there was an accepted set of norms. If we had stayed, and if we never broke the rules, we might never have felt uneasy. But God had called us out of our comfort zone, into the unfamiliar, in order to reach a people for Jesus.

I mistakenly thought that since Christ sent me to La Sabana, it was now my responsibility to bring the Muinanes to a knowledge of God. I failed to understand that God gave *Christ* the responsibility to redeem the world. He never asked me to take on the responsibility for redeeming the Muinanes. He was trying to tell me, "It is not your responsibility, Jim; it is mine." He merely wanted me to place myself in the yoke next to himself. I would find no rest until I shouldered his yoke, for then Christ would be next to me, and he would be pulling the load.

Instead, I tried to pull my own yoke. And it didn't work very well. I often felt pulled between family and ministry, between choices that no one should be asked to make.

Jan's health problems resulted in multiple surgeries during our years in Colombia. One such operation came during Diana's senior year in high school. Jan was still in the hospital in Bogotá when Diana came down with malaria in Lomalinda. I didn't want to leave Jan's hospital bed; neither was it fair to leave others to care for my daughter, whose body was racked with fever and chills. Diana was staying at the home of Fred and Esther Gross, who were taking marvelous care of her, but I felt that

Diana needed to see one of her parents. I also feared that if I did not come to see her, she might imagine her mother's illness to be even more critical than it was. Traveling the 150 miles between Bogotá and Lomalinda was expensive and tiring, but there was no way I could leave either of them alone.

Through it all, God was faithful. I couldn't be in two places at one time, but God could. I had to trust that God loved Jan and Diana even more than I did, and he was with them even when I couldn't be. Still, it was an extremely painful and difficult time for all of us.

I had committed my life to serving God. It had taken me to the jungles, and it was becoming more than I had bargained for. I was learning that, not only do Christians get sick, but sickness can debilitate one's spirit as well as the body. Good people die, as well as bad ones. Missionaries are martyred. I accepted that, but at times I still struggled. Jean Nicolas Grou writes, "The chief pang of most trials is not so much the suffering itself, as our own spirit of resistance to it."

I believe God is sovereign. He may leave things in our path to cause us to return to him. I believe nothing strikes us but what has been filtered through God's grace, love, and mercy. The account of Joseph being sold into slavery in Egypt clearly tells us that God often uses what is meant for evil for our good, if we are able to accept it. He can use sickness for his glory and our growth. Saying this in a church meeting is one thing; believing it in life's jungles is another.

Life was closing in and crashing down on me. I knew deep inside the quietness of my mind that this was all part of the calling I was born to fulfill, and it would pass. Yet the harsh, noisy circumstances of life seemed to shout, *Don't you remember that Jan almost died from who knows what, Diana from malaria, and Danny from hepatitis? Diana almost lost her sight from that severe eye infection, remember? Isn't that enough?* The devil was trying to tell me that it didn't have to be this way.

It wasn't that God was not at work. It wasn't that I believed the devil's lies, or that I doubted the necessity of what we were doing. But the toll on my family was more than I could take. I was sure that if we stayed, somebody would die. I was tired, the people were upset with me because I didn't bring them salt on the last flight, and the gnats were driving me crazy!

I descended the board steps of our jungle home, crossed the dirt patio, and walked to the airstrip. The tropical, midday sun was intense, and I looked toward the shade and cover of the trail leading into the jungle. But I turned instead to the open airstrip. I wanted no thick canopy of trees to shelter me from the sun; I was about to shout to heaven, and nothing must interfere!

Slowly, I walked the length of the grassy airstrip— muttering, complaining, struggling with God and my thoughts every step of the way. Back and forth across the 450-meter airstrip, I argued with God. I reasoned, I shouted, I cried, I screamed. *I've been here long enough, God. Let somebody else come!* Like Christ's disciples in the storm, I wanted Christ to step into my boat and calm the raging winds. But I felt as if Christ were still watching me from a Galilean hillside, far away. I wanted him right beside me, making the storm disappear. The going was getting rough, and I felt a longing to get going. Finally, I cried, "God, I want to go home!"

It is hard to hear the still small voice of God until the noise of the earthquake, fire, and wind have died. Was the voice not there all the time? I think it was. God spoke the same words to Elijah before the storm as after the storm (1 Kings 19:9, 13). Could his voice not have been heard in the midst of the storm?

Like Elijah, and everyone since, I would find that after the earthquake, the thunder, the fire, and the worst that life can throw at us, there remains the quiet voice of God. I'm still trying to train my soul to pick out God's voice in the midst of life's storms. Until then, I know that after the storm, God will always be there, waiting to pick me up and carry me forward. God understands our fears, our emotional and spiritual frame. He gently nurtures and nudges us to help us grow in obedience. He always works at our pace, and only as we are willing to trust him for another step.

For one brief moment, I knew, at the core of my being, why this place was called "the river that God forgot." Then, as soon as I cried out my frustration to God, I was overcome by an outpouring of God's peace. God didn't calm the storms of life, but he calmed the storms in me. Christ had joined me in the boat, and I knew I would not drown.

I climbed the steps back up into our jungle home with a lighter heart. The roof still leaked, smoke from the fire in the mud stove still filled the air, rats still ran on the poles overhead, and the gnats—the ever-present gnats— swarmed around my head. I knew that life in the jungle might never be easy, but I knew it was good—because it was right.

Jan and the children agree that those years, though difficult, were good years for us. We shared them as a family; we shared the work, the challenges, and the blessings. Our children were as much a part of the translation and the Muinane work as Jan or I. Still, we wanted to know what Diana and Dan would say about their childhood, if we asked them today. And so we asked. Here is what they wrote:

DIANA—1992

Good Things about My Growing Up in Colombia:
- It stimulated my creativeness or inventive side, as there was no "packaged" entertainment.
- The experience of living in another culture and learning another language expanded my horizons and opened my heart to a whole different world and awareness of others.

Bad Things about My Growing Up in Colombia:
- Not getting to know my grandparents very well.
- The only glimpse I had of death was the wailing of the Indians' hopelessness.
- I was scared of the outhouse, especially at night— the bats, snakes, and jaguars that I just *knew* were out there.

How I Feel about Having Grown Up in Colombia:
- I wouldn't trade growing up in Colombia for anything in the whole world. It's what I have

always wanted for my children. As I talk with friends who have never had the special privilege of experiencing life from other than an American perspective, I thank God for taking us to Colombia—I can't imagine life any different.

DAN—1992

Good Things about My Growing Up in Colombia:
- I was taught valuable lessons about God's love for other people, who were not exactly like me; and I was taught that God loved me too.
- I learned that sacrificing wasn't necessarily negative. We didn't have everything, but we had everything we needed.

Bad Things about My Growing Up in Colombia:
- Maybe I wasn't as close to my relatives, as I might have otherwise been if I had grown up stateside.

How I Feel about Having Grown Up in Colombia:
- I would not forfeit the opportunity of having grown up in Colombia for anything. As a child, I had the perfect playground. I had a wonderful family and nothing to worry about.

These testimonies from our children helped seal our assurance that it was right to stay and weather the storms. Our greatest struggle had been how our ministry would affect our children. But, as always, God knew exactly what he was doing.

Years after my encounter with God on the airstrip,

God gave me another assurance. I was walking to the village with a young Muinane man. As we crossed the airstrip, the site of my spiritual battle, the man stopped. He placed a hand on my shoulder and said, "Jim, thanks for coming to La Sabana and bringing us Jesus." He turned, and we walked on to the village with those few quiet words ringing in my heart. I still hear them echo today.

The jungle of Colombia held many threats to our safety: dangerous animals, strange diseases, challenges to our faith. Perhaps your jungle holds different dangers, threats we have never known or experienced. But the Lord who was faithful to us in our jungle will be faithful to you in yours. You can do more than just survive. You can conquer the jungle and all its jaguars through the holy blood of the Lamb.

CHAPTER ELEVEN

Darkness and Demons

The timid it concerns to ask their way,
And fear what foe in caves and swamps can stray,
To make no step until the event is known,
And ills to come as evils past bemoan.
— Ralph Waldo Emerson

JIM'S STORY

Five-year-old Selimo didn't show up for class one day. When questioned about his absence, he explained, "On my way to school I was met by the devil and he said, 'Selimo, don't go to school today.' So I played until school was over and it was time to go home."

The Muinanes had no problem believing in the devil, for their culture is filled with superstitions, omens, and evil spirits. But I don't think anyone believed Selimo that day. The devil was merely his excuse for doing what he knew was wrong.

I wonder how often we try to blame the devil for our own sins. Perhaps it was the demon of anger, the demon of lust, the demon of this, or the demon of that. "The devil made me do it," we say, when really it was the "Selimo" inside us who wanted to disobey.

I have always believed in demons—sort of. Before going to South America, I can't recall any major direct contact or confrontations with demons, but I still believed they existed. Over the years, I had experienced the typical problems, difficulties, and inconveniences that attacked me when preparing a sermon on the devil or studying about his wiles. At key points of ministry, and at the start or end of some significant spiritual program or event, everything seemed to go wrong: equipment would break, illness would strike, and troubles would multiply. I considered these things to be demonic or Satanic attacks to delay and prevent the work of God. My belief in the occult, however, was a little vague and rather distant. Demons were real, but I considered them more of a nuisance than a threat.

The first time I heard the audible voice of a demon, I thought I was dreaming. I hoped I was dreaming. I prayed that I was dreaming. It was no dream.

I had gone to La Sabana alone—one of the very few times I did so. Jan was sick, no one else was free to go with me, and it was important that I go. I had retired early that night and soon was sound asleep.

I have never suffered from insomnia. If I need sleep, I sleep; if I wake up in the night, there must be something better to do than sleep, or I would be sleeping. I seldom get out of bed, but I find that the night hours are a wonderful time to solve problems and to meditate. Some of my most uncluttered, unencumbered, uninterrupted hours are in the night. The Scriptures say that the righ-

teous are to "meditate [in God's Law] day and night."
For my part, I do not want to fret away my best hours to
meditate by labeling them as insomnia.

On the other hand, if I am tired, I sleep quite soundly.
Anyone who has ever slept in the same house with me
can attest to that fact. A friend once removed the mattress from his bed, moved down the hall, and slept on the
bathroom floor because of my snoring.

What was it that physically startled me awake in the
middle of the night when I was alone in our jungle home?
I don't remember any movement. I heard no strange
sounds except those of the jungle, and I had already come
to recognize and appreciate many of the nocturnal noises.
I sensed an ominous presence there with me, but I could
not see anyone. Then a voice pierced the darkness. "Who
are you? And why are you here?" it demanded.

I shook my head to clear my imagination and wake my
senses. Then I realized that I was awake—wide awake.
My senses were vibrant, and I felt like a bundle of raw
nerve endings, recoiling from a solid, brutal sense of
something or someone in the room. Again the voice
demanded, "Who are you?"

Did I dare answer? Did I dare not answer? Did I have
a choice? Frantic thoughts began crashing against each
other in a mad scramble to find answers, to bring some
reason to the madness that surrounded me. I took a deep
breath and answered the question. "Jim Walton. I'm Jim
Walton." I let my breath out slow—*wheeeeew!* Surely that
was the end of the dream.

The voice continued and insisted, "But *who* are you?
And what are you doing here?" I had heard stories of

familiar spirits and shaman powers, of Martin Luther throwing an ink bottle at the devil, of the evil spirits who begged Christ to send them into a herd of pigs. I had heard of ghosts and goblins and witches. *What's happening here?* I asked silently. *Am I crazy? Is this Halloween? Is this an extremely vivid, bad dream? What am I doing, trying to talk to a demon—if, of course, that's what it is?*

I sat up, took another breath, and tried to take charge of my emotions and the situation. But before I could say another word, the voice repeated the question. I felt thrown back onto the bed—whether by fear or something stronger, I cannot say.

Again and again I tried to answer, but still the question was repeated. I tried Spanish: "Me llamo Jaime Walton." I tried Muinane: "Uujoho T++faibo." Still the spirit voice was not satisfied. It kept insisting, *"Who* are you? And what are you doing here?"

Terrified, I called silently to God for help. I suddenly realized that the voice was not asking for my name. The voice was asking me to identify who I was internally, what business I had living in that part of the jungle, and what I was truly about. I answered, "It doesn't matter who I am. I belong to Jesus, and he sent me here to do his work." That was it—the voice, the "being" was gone! Never again, in eighteen years, did that same voice— whether spirit or demon—return.

For years I told no one of this encounter because I didn't want to risk facing people's skepticism or mockery. Some might think I was dreaming, while others might doubt my memory—or even my sanity! It was also a time when some saw a jaguar behind every tree, a snake under every rock, and a demon in every sin. I was afraid of my own and everybody else's doctrines about the occult. It could be argued today that the church has advanced in its views, or maybe it is I who has matured. Few today fail to admit that we are involved in a very real spiritual warfare. Paul wrote, "We wrestle not against flesh and blood, but against principalities, against powers, against the rulers of the darkness of this world, against spiritual wickedness in high places" (Eph. 6:12).

I do not wish, by writing this, to add to the confusion surrounding the occult. But the story of the Muinanes is incomplete without it, for their culture includes the occult with its myths, superstitions, and supernatural phenomenon. We pass off most superstition as false, but few of us would deny that the occult world exists. A part of me is still skeptical; yet another part of me says, "Maybe there is something more than I want to admit."

One person may consider a particular occurrence as clear proof of demonic forces, yet the next individual might dismiss it as pure coincidence. C. S. Lewis writes, "There are two equal and opposite errors into which our race can fall about the devils. One is to disbelieve in their existence. The other is to believe, and to feel an excessive and unhealthy interest in them. They themselves are equally pleased by both errors" (C. S. Lewis, *The Screwtape Letters* [New York: Macmillan, 1957]).

When Danny was about six years old, he developed a round white spot about the size of a quarter on his cheek. All the pigment disappeared from that spot for no apparent reason. Several months passed, and one day Clementina's grandmother, Magdalena, sat looking intently at

Danny's face. Suddenly she walked across the porch, grabbed Danny and bit him, leaving teeth marks around the white spot on his face. Everyone was surprised, but none more than Danny, who ran screaming to his mother. Magdalena just kept saying, "I can't believe anybody would curse little Danny. Who could have done it?" She explained that the white spot was caused by a curse and that the "evil spirit" had to be driven out of the spot or a worse fate would follow.

Danny wasn't convinced that biting was the best way to handle the situation! And we weren't at all convinced that the spot on his cheek had anything to do with the spirit world. Magdalena, however, viewed it as unquestionable validation of her belief when the white spot disappeared and the pigment returned.

Most of us allow ourselves to take what suits us from both the physical world and the supernatural. We seek an eclectic sort of marriage between the seen and the unseen, the material and the spiritual. Some events do not make much sense if the world is only rational in a physical sense. Even here caution is prudent, since it is as easy to become excessively superstitious as it is to be excessively rationalistic.

One day Alicia was distraught as she stopped to visit on her way to her garden. "Something awful has happened. Someone in my family has died."

"How do you know?" I asked. "Did someone arrive with the news?"

"No, but they will be coming. The evil spirits told me so last night."

When we asked for an explanation, Alicia spoke of the

"swinging hammock." Hammocks typically swing from side to side, as one would imagine, from the wind or body movement or someone pushing against it. The type of swinging Alicia spoke of was an omen of impending death: In the middle of the night, when all is silent in the *maloka* and darkness prevails, a hammock will move as if someone, or something, has taken hold of the ropes at each end of the hammock. The rope becomes taut, lifting the hammock and the weight of the person's body upwards. Then, slowly, the hammock and the person in it are let back down. Up and down, again and again it moves, but no one is touching the ropes.

According to Alicia and the rest of the Muinanes, the phenomenon occurs only when somone is about to die. It happens selectively — to the person or persons most closely involved or affected by the death. It sometimes happens when the recipient of the omen knows about the sickness. More strangely, it happens when someone a great distance from the village dies, someone who was not known to be sick.

Within a few days, messengers from Alicia's family arrived at La Sabana with news of the death of one of her relatives. We thought it a strange coincidence and dismissed the incident. Then, years later, we heard another story that made us think again.

On a Sunday evening at Lomalinda, Joel Stolte, translator for the Northern Barasano people, was giving a report on a recent trip that he had taken. Soon after arriving at the village, Joel had learned that a small child was sick. The symptoms indicated pneumonia, which could be treated with antibiotics. But the child's parents

141

said that they had taken the child to the shaman, who had consulted with the spirits. The child would die. "There is nothing to do," the parents submitted.

Joel pled with the parents and the shaman, "Please let me give some medicine to the child. It will save his life." The parents and shaman reluctantly gave permission, but the shaman assured Joel, "The spirits have already announced the child's death."

I had been listening intently, but I bolted upright in my seat when I heard Joel's next statement. "That night I was awakened by the swinging of my hammock. I lay very still to detect if there might be a breeze that would cause the hammock to move. Nothing! Then the hammock seemed to move upward, as if someone was at each end of the hammock, pulling the ropes straight back. I looked into the darkness, but no one was there!" Joel went on to tell about the darkness, the oppression, and his uneasiness, but *my* mind was racing in another direction. I had brushed Alicia's story away as a coincidence, superstition, but here was another, a *missionary*, saying he had experienced the exact same thing. Could this be real?

The last words I remember Joel speaking were, "The child died."

The Muinanes and the Northern Barasanos are geographically, culturally, and linguistically separated. Puzzling? Yes, but there are people groups, some half a world apart, who, like the Muinanes and the Barasanos, have different cultures, mutually unintelligible languages, have never met, are totally unaware that the other group exists—yet they share the same omens. Is this total coincidence?

Through the years that we lived with the Muinanes, we encountered more coincidences and strange encounters with the spirit world. Mark Anderson, a friend from Minnesota, was visiting us. One night he and I decided to head off into the jungle to do some hunting. Jan was alone in the house when, from the far end of the airstrip, the peaceful night sounds of the jungle and the darkness were shattered. Jan heard strange noises that sounded like the voice of a woman being chased and screaming. The screaming continued until "she" reached a point directly in line with the house where Jan sat with only a candle for light. Then there was nothing! Nothing except darkness and silence and mystery.

Unaware of what had happened, Mark and I returned, empty-handed, from hunting. We neither saw nor heard anything out of the ordinary. The Muinanes who lived a short distance from the end of the airstrip, however, heard the ominous sounds. The next day they told us which demon it was and the reason for its appearance. Incredulous, I inquired if the spirit had the form of an animal or if there was an animal in the jungle that looked like this "demon" or that made a similar sound—surely there must be a natural explanation! Not so; or if there was, we never learned it.

The Muinanes lived in fear of many demons: the patron spirits of foods, the owner-spirits of the wild pigs and the jaguar, and any of a multitude of spirits. I regarded much of what was happening as superstition or unreasonable, and it made little difference when I was confronted with evidence that I did not care to believe. So much was clearly myth and superstition that I was reluctant to attribute demonic forces to things that might later prove no more plausible than a rabbit's foot or a lucky penny. But later events left little doubt about the forces with which we were dealing.

Jan had undergone major surgery, and our return to La Sabana was delayed. The Lord, however, supplied daily strength and we returned sooner than expected. Upon arriving in La Sabana, we found that Satan, who could not triumph by bringing sickness to the translators, had begun concentrating on the Muinanes through curses, unexplained deaths, personal manifestations, and fear.

One woman in the village, María, saw and talked with two unknown "spirit beings" that said they were sent as a curse to her and her husband. They followed her for two hours back along the trail through the jungle to her house. María told her husband of the strange visit, then went to sleep that night. She arose the next day and went about her normal work, showing no signs of sickness or fatigue. She lay down in her hammock for a rest in the middle of the morning, and in a few minutes she was dead. A few days later a tree fell on her husband, Ramón, breaking his cheekbone, driving his upper teeth into the gumline, knocking him unconscious, and causing temporary loss of hearing. He lived in constant fear, as everyday tasks brought frequent unexplained injury and he, as well as others, were visited by the "evil spirits."

One such visit came after we asked him to come to our house and help us check the first few verses we had completed in our draft of the translation of 1 John.

Ramón promised to return the following day, but that night he was visited by four evil spirits warning him of danger and death that awaited him if he left his home the next day.

It was becoming harder to say that all the things that were happening were mere accidental responses to particular actions. We began to wonder if this cycle was being repeated by total chance. I was becoming more willing to concede that superstition was not a thing of the past; and it was not confined to the less educated.

Much superstition is concerned with good or bad luck, either as omens or practices that supposedly offer protection. Examples from our own culture include: breaking mirrors, spilling salt, stepping on cracks, knocking on wood, a horseshoe, a rabbit's foot, charms, amulets, crystals, and so on. I knew that a great part of superstition was a fear of the unknown, a trust in magic or chance, or a false conception of causation. Much of what is found in primitive societies, and even in our own so-called sophisticated society, is due to false interpretations, inadequate observation, or selective forgetfulness; but these do not give a full accounting of the supernatural.

At some point, it becomes impossible to dismiss all these events as nothing more than chance. If I treat all superstition as an error in reasoning or a delusion, I must then ask myself, how is it possible that the delusion persists? Might Satan use some of these beliefs, superstitions, and omens, and even influence their outcome in order to keep an individual or society in bondage? The apostle Paul indicates that this is true: "The god of this world hath blinded the minds of them which believe not, lest the light of the glorious gospel of Christ, who is the image of God, should shine unto them" (2 Cor. 4:4). Paul also warned Timothy that "some shall depart from the faith, giving heed to seducing spirits, and doctrines of devils" (1 Tim. 4:1).

We need to know our enemy; the hardest enemy to defeat is the one we do not recognize. The Muinanes are very aware of their natural enemies. More than any animal, they fear the snake that lies silent, unnoticed, by the side of the trail, hidden in the grass, or in the dark corners of the house. Likewise, we must be aware of our spiritual enemies, those forces that are fighting against our efforts and challenging our authority as agents of Jesus Christ.

I was summoned to "come quickly" one Sunday afternoon because a Muinane man was being attacked by demons. I arrived to find Alejandro writhing in his hammock, crying and screaming for the devils to leave him alone. "Go away! I do not belong to you," he shouted. "I don't hear [obey] you anymore. Go! Get away! Stop torturing me!" Then, weak and fighting, he bolted, as if pulled from the hammock, and threw himself, moaning and screaming, into the fire. The men had wrestled Alejandro back into the hammock several times. This time they called for me and said, "Jim, do something; the devils are going to kill him!"

The position of the sun told me that it was only midday, but I felt as if the whole village was in darkness. I had nowhere to run, nowhere to hide. It was too late to avoid the confrontation, yet I knew the forces besetting Alejandro were greater than my strength. I was scared! I don't remember my exact thoughts, but I was not the oft portrayed "brave young Christian warrior" eager to do battle with demonic forces. I just did what I had to do in the face of uncertainty, and in spite of my fears.

Mostly I prayed. I remember helping pull Alejandro away from the fire and, with my arm around him, leading him back to his hammock. I continued to pray. After some time, I realized that the heaviness that had covered the village had disappeared. The demonic forces subsided.

Some may think, *What a marvelous experience.* Yes, it was; but when demons are real, it can also be an exhausting, terrifying experience. Marvelous are the words of Christ to his disciples, "Rejoice not that the spirits are subject unto you; but rather rejoice, because your names are written in heaven" (Luke 10:20).

At times we may tremble before the occult or be tempted to cower in fear of demonic darkness. But we, like the Muinanes, are learning that we need fear no evil, for God is with us. We do not know each step that God has mapped out for our lives. We do not know what evil waits beside the path, but we do know that God's love foreshadows our way. His word is a lamp unto our feet and a light unto our path.

So if someone, or even the devil himself, asks you, "Who are you?" I pray that you can answer, "I am a child of God."

And I pray when they ask us, "What are you doing here?" we can tell them we have been commanded to "shine like stars in the universe" as we "hold out the word of life" (Phil. 2:15-16, NIV).

We do not fight against flesh and blood, but neither do

we fight with mere muscles and bones. We fight with the shield of faith and the sword of the Spirit. And we are already promised the victory.

CHAPTER TWELVE

Speaking the Truth in Love

Though Love repine, and Reason chafe
There came a voice without reply,
'Tis man's perdition to be safe,
When for the truth he ought to die.
    —R. W. Emerson

JAN'S STORY

On July 20, 1969, most of the world waited expectantly in front of television screens. A man was about to walk on the moon for the first time. Deep in the Amazon jungle, a few miles from the imaginary line that marks the center of the earth, a few young Muinane men listened on a small transistor radio.

A few minutes later, these young men climbed the steps to our jungle home, full of questions. Where in the sky are the sun, moon, and the stars? How did they get there?

We talked about the universe, planets, groups of stars called galaxies, and the God who set them all in place. As we talked, Jim illustrated our solar system by means of a basketball, a caimo fruit, and a grape. Does that remind you of your school days?

That night, as perhaps in every home around the world, the topic of discussion around the flickering fires of the Muinanes was, "One small step for a man. One giant leap for mankind."

Very early the next day, with the sun's rays still filtering through the morning fog, Magdalena came to ask us about the strange rumors of the night before. "Is it true that your people went up to the moon?"

We saw the pleading in her eyes, the hope that we would not confirm the young men's foolish tales. We answered as kindly and gently as we could. "We know it seems strange, Magdalena, but the stories are true. A man has flown to the moon."

"This American stepped on him?" she gasped. "What did he say?"

For more than seventy years she had mistaken the creation for the Creator. She had placed her faith and her eternal destiny in a round ball suspended in the universe. Her god was no god at all. She had been deceived into thinking there was life and hope in a planet that consisted merely of dust and rock, craters and barrenness. She had observed the lights in the sky, but had never been told of the God who had created the heavenly lights. Thousands of years before, God had warned Israel, "And when you look up to the sky and see the sun, the moon and the stars—all the heavenly array—do not be enticed into bowing down to them and worshiping" (Deut. 4:19, NIV).

But even if we risked offending her, we had to tell

Magdalena the truth. "The moon didn't talk, Magdalena, because it is not alive. The moon is not a god. The moon was created by God."

For a time, Magdalena wasn't sure what to believe—so many strange ideas, difficult to understand, hard to accept. When the rains were delayed, she was sure it was because our relatives had stepped on the moon and made "him" angry.

Eventually Magdalena did come to believe in the Creator God. She was led to faith in Christ through one of her grandchildren. At the moment of her new birth, a new life began and old things began passing away. Many of the old beliefs disappeared slowly as she grew in her knowledge of the truth. We had taken the risk to speak the truth in love.

Some people want to insulate such cultures from outside contact in order to preserve the cultural heritage. But whether we tell them the truth or not, these cultures are being, and will continue to be, confronted with the outside world—the good and the bad, with lies and with truth. We believe that we must tell them the truth, as we did with Magdalena—both the truth about the universe, and the God who created it. Anything less would be unfair to them, unfair to the truth itself. Truth will confirm truth, and truth will destroy myth.

All known primitive cultures are religious. They may worship the jaguar, the snake, or the moon, but they believe in the supernatural. If the moon is god, then god is destroyed when people discover the moon's true nature. This creates a vacuum in people's hearts. The vacuum must be filled, or the structure will collapse with horrifying effects on the culture. We felt compelled to fill those vacuums, to tell the Muinanes about the one true God, and to instruct them in the Christian way—to make disciples.

In the Old Testament, God announced his missionary objective in a promise to Abraham: "I will surely bless you and make your descendants as numerous as the stars in the sky and as the sand on the seashore. Your descendants will take possession of the cities of their enemies, and through your offspring all nations on earth will be blessed, because you have obeyed me" (Gen. 22:17-18, NIV). In the New Testament, the apostle Paul reinforced the call to speak the truth in love when he reminded the Galatian Christians that "the Scriptures looked forward to this time when God would save the Gentiles also, through their faith" (Gal. 3:8, TLB). And Jesus told his followers to "Go into all the world and preach the good news to all creation" (Mark 16:15, NIV).

Christianity and correct cross-cultural ministry do not destroy cultures. The Christian faith will not only thrive and grow within any culture, but will strengthen and enhance it. The truth, spoken in love, enriches every culture and every individual who embraces it.

One day Virgelina, an eighteen-year-old Muinane girl, reminded me of the importance of our calling. Virgelina was a friend of our daughter, Diana, who was away at school in Lomalinda. "Could I send Diana a letter?" Virgelina asked. "Is there some way I could send a gift to her? What can I send?"

I thought for a moment about the relationship between the two girls, and I realized that with Virgelina, love was the key. "Diana loves you so much," I told the girl at last, "and the best gift you could send to her would be news that you had opened your heart to Jesus."

Virgelina immediately replied, "That's why I've come. I want Jesus to be my Savior. Will you help me pray?"

Because we had spoken truth to the Muinanes, a new spiritual life was born, and two girls who had been friends became sisters, with an eternal bond in Christ.

Our efforts to bring truth to the Muinanes were necessarily limited by many external and internal constraints. Because of our specialized ministry and agreements with our host country, our work was nonsectarian and nonecclesiastical. We could do no formal preaching, teaching, or evangelism. Our teaching was done one on one, at the kitchen stove, or on the porch.

At night the young men came, one by one or with a friend, to ask questions about the world, about big cities, about the stars that hang in the heavens, and much more. We tried to answer their questions the best we could and use the opportunities God gave us to tell the Muinanes about Christ. We also taught at the translation desk as we discussed the meaning of the words and verses we translated.

One of our greatest thrills came when, after checking a number of very difficult verses, Jim asked one of the young men, "It's a hard passage, isn't it?"

The man responded, "Yes, it is hard, but I understand it because it's in my language."

After we had translated eight Bible stories, Andrés recorded them onto a cassette tape. The people often gathered on our porch to listen to the little talking box

153

that spoke their language. The people's responses were varied: Some merely listened, others discussed, a few would turn and walk away. We knew for certain that Chief Fernando was listening carefully, for one day he responded, "This is all true! I know it is, but not one of us does what it says."

We often recalled his statement as we continued to translate the Scriptures. We could not expect the Muinanes to believe what the Bible told them if they did not see these truths lived out in our own lives. Speaking the truth must always be accompanied by living the truth.

When Christ walked the earth, he found many different ways to speak the truth, but he always spoke the language of the people. He often used everyday situations and circumstances as an opportunity to teach his disciples:

> He told them that the kingdom of God is like a field,
>   a pearl of great price, a treasure,
>   a net.
> He taught giving, by the widow's mite,
>   watchfulness, by the lamps,
>   obedience, by suffering and death,
>   faith, by a little seed.
> He used a wedding feast,
>   a lamp under a basket,
>   a loaf of bread and a few fish,
>   a foundation, solid or sandy,
>   a lost sheep,
>   a lost coin.

I don't read anywhere that Christ ever used the example of a cookie sheet, but it was through a cookie sheet that we taught an important lesson.

After one of our visits to Lomalinda, we returned to the village to discover that our cookie sheet was missing. It was just an old cookie sheet, nine inches square, black from smoke, and bent from packing it away in a barrel or box each time we left the jungle. It wasn't worth much, and if we could have bought another, we would have thrown it away.

But that bent cookie sheet was all we had, and it was just the right size to fit into our very small oven. We often remarked that it reminded us of ourselves. What a team to send to a tribe with a tonal language in the Amazon jungle—one was tone deaf, the other couldn't swim. But we were the only ones God had sent to the Muinanes.

Rumor was usually pinpoint accurate in the small village, and this time it pointed to one young man. In the Muinane culture there are some right ways and many wrong ways to confront people. Did we want to take the risk? After all, it was just a cookie sheet. Jim and I decided that the biscuits I baked on the cookie sheet might not be that important, but the lesson *was* important.

The right opportunity came shortly before one of the Muinanes' all-night festivals. I was talking with the suspected cookie-sheet thief. I told him about the missing cookie sheet and that, even though it was old and of little value, it was the only one that would fit into our little oven. I told him I was sad because I couldn't bake biscuits for my family. Then I asked the young man to check around the village and help me get it back.

The night of the festival, the whole village was together in one house. During the night, the young man slipped away. When the others noticed he was gone, they warned us that he was likely breaking into our house again. It was too far and too late to return home that night. It wasn't long, however, before the young man came back.

We returned home the next day and our house had been entered, but we found nothing missing. When I opened the cupboard, I found the little cookie sheet right where it belonged. Fellowship was restored. The young man once again had "one heart": he was at peace. A simple lesson of honesty and relationships was taught by means of a cookie sheet.

One warm tropical evening, five years after our first entrance into the tribe, Arturo came to join Jim on the porch of our palm-bark house. I left them alone to visit, but I could hear much of their conversation through the split-palm walls of our home — and the rest of it, Jim eagerly repeated to me after Arturo left.

Arturo selected a *National Geographic* magazine from the shelf as if he were choosing a specific book in a huge library. He leafed through the pages quickly and placed his finger at a certain page. He kept this place in the magazine as they talked about many things, from the people who were sick to the new house that was being built in the village. It was evident that something more was on Arturo's mind.

Arturo had a mixed reputation in the village, but since our arriving back this time, his actions had changed noticeably. His speech was quiet, more agreeable and polite. He even helped his wife carry her baskets of manioc and firewood. Perhaps the example of the chief, who had started helping his wife after he became a Christian, was affecting Arturo's habits.

Knowing Jim as I do, I imagine he was nearly bursting with curiosity by the time Arturo finally, after two hours, opened the magazine. "What are these people in this picture doing?" Arturo asked abruptly, as he held up the magazine to the light of the candle for Jim to see.

The picture portrayed a bountiful table of food with a family bowing in grateful thanks to God, the giver of all good things. Before Jim could phrase an answer, Arturo rushed on, "Are they praying?"

In the Muinanes' mind, praying is associated with being a Christian. Instead of referring directly to the picture, Jim asked point blank, "Arturo, do you want to ask God to make you one of his children?"

Arturo's answer was quick and clear. "I have! I am already a believer."

Arturo unfolded the story of how he had placed his faith in Christ. "After you left from your last visit to La Sabana, I obtained a Spanish Bible and took it to the jungle to read. I did not understand it all, but I found many words I knew, and those words told me that this God of the Bible is the true God. I came back to my house believing in God."

"This is wonderful!" Jim exclaimed. "What about your wife? Have you told her about your new faith?"

"Yes, she believes too. Every evening when we get into our hammocks, I make God's words talk to her and to our children. Then I talk with God."

We were overjoyed. We considered framing the picture

that gave Arturo the courage to tell us how the Lord had saved him. Instead, it remained in the magazine on the shelf where other Muinanes might see it and wonder, *What are they doing?*

As one by one the Muinanes turned to Christ, some began to ask about meeting together to study God's Word and sing the songs of Jesus. But where would they meet, and who would lead the services? It would have been easy to expect the white missionaries to lead the services at the missionaries' house. But we could not, and we felt we should not. If the services were at our house, where would they meet when we were away from the village? And what would they do once we were gone for good?

Because the Muinanes were a small group, it was conceivable that we could evangelize the whole tribe. But even if we could reach every Muinane, we knew that we could not stay forever. After providing the Muinanes with the New Testament and encouraging them to grow and build on the foundation of their new faith, we would move on. We would reinvest our lives elsewhere in God's service and would expect the Muinane believers to continue the work begun among their people. Who would teach God's Word to future generations? We felt our task was to plant seeds that would grow and reproduce from within the Muinane culture.

We wanted the Muinanes to become responsible for the spread and growth of the gospel among their people and their neighbors. We wanted to help them understand that God had a plan for their lives, and help them discover how they fit into God's family. For all these reasons, we could not help too much with their Bible studies. The Muinanes must decide where they would meet, and one of them could lead the services.

Soon the Muinanes were meeting to study God's Word in their homes. Often the designated leader would be one of the young men who had worked with us on the translation. They might choose some verses from the Spanish Bible and come to our house, the day or night before, to go over and discuss the meaning of the verses. As time went on, some chose to explain the verses we had translated into Muinane that week. Through honoring our nonsectarian, nonecclesiastical pledge, we were obeying the conditions of our contract with the nation, and we allowed the Muinanes to find culturally relevant expressions of the Christian faith.

As more of the people came to believe in God, we realized that some of their experiences would prove to be genuine and lasting. But other people would be like the seed that fell on rocky soil—springing up quickly but dying from lack of roots.

We knew that some would encounter this new teaching and begin to question their previous beliefs. They would feel the poverty of their religious assumptions and wonder if they wanted to continue living in the same meaningless routine. They might be tired of fearing the evil spirits and so might turn to a new religion. But if there is no repentance, no real concern about sin, no turning to God for salvation, then there is no genuine commitment. Even if they swept and cleaned up their own lives, they would still be empty without Christ.

The devil would not care if a Muinane changed religions. He might even withdraw for a time, and allow the person to reform his life and enter into the fellowship of Christians—as long as it was not real. The devil is unafraid of reform so long as there is no true commitment and acceptance of Christ and his salvation. In a little while the devil will return to find the person empty.

We were well aware that we were engaged in an act of aggression: we were intruding upon the devil's territory. Satan and his hosts had ruled this river—this "river that God forgot"—virtually uncontested for thousands of years. Satan opposed our efforts, and when someone would accept the gospel, he would seek to lure them away from following God.

One of Satan's greatest tools to turn people's hearts away from God is worldly possessions. We might expect this in London, Munich, Tokyo, or Dallas—but La Sabana? The Muinanes had never had many worldly goods. Would they also be tempted by riches and things? Amazing as it may seem, the human heart is the same in every culture and every land.

The world that had given so little to the Muinanes now seemed to offer them riches at little cost. Drug lords, in search of the world's finest cocaine, brought the devil's promises of money, riches, and earthly goods far into the jungles of Peru, Bolivia, and Colombia. Those who have lived in a rich, affluent society might realize the folly and deceitfulness of money and things. The Muinanes had never had a chance to be rich in terms of worldly goods. This was their one big opportunity at wealth.

While feeling sad for the Muinanes and trying to instruct them in scriptural values concerning life, posses-sions, and money, we had to reexamine our own devotion to God. We found that too often our own hearts are set on earthly goods. The Scriptures warn, "If riches increase, set not your heart upon them" (Ps. 62:10). And the apostle John wrote that we are not to try to combine devotion to the world's things with loyalty to Christ.

C. S. Lewis expressed the following insight in *The Screwtape Letters:* "Prosperity knits a man to the World. He feels that he is 'finding his place in it,' while really it is finding its place in him."

All too often luxuries become necessities; the more we get, the more we need. There is always one more thing that we think we can't live without. Someday we will step into eternity, alongside our Muinane brothers and sisters. We will all stand stripped of our earthly possessions. Someone else will inherit their canoes and our cars, and all the trinkets we amassed on earth. Our earthly possessions will count for absolutely nothing in that place. Our faith in God and our relationship with Christ must always be our most valued possessions.

During our early years with the Muinanes, some came to another mistaken notion, that the Christian life was meant to make one perpetually happy. They began to think that it was God's obligation to shield Christians from everything painful, disagreeable, or upsetting. It came as a shock to some that God would allow us and our children to become sick. It still comes as a shock to some of us that God's primary purpose for us is not to make us rich or comfortable, but to conform us to the image of his Son.

The goal of the disciple is to become like Christ, but it is no more possible for us to transform ourselves into his image by striving to imitate him than for the Muinanes to become Christians by mimicking the foreigner's form of worship and adopting his standards of conduct. Rather, Christ needs to be formed in us. This is a glorious picture, but often a painful process. To become like Christ, we must be conformed to his death. It is not easy to die to self.

One young Muinane believer was wronged and openly set about to seek revenge. Revenge for the Muinanes was not passive, but vindictive and injurious. We asked the young believer about his determination to retaliate. "It is the law of the jungle," he replied. "I am entitled to get my payback. After I do that, I will forgive."

We tried to explain that Christians are to forgive and let God worry about paying back. We shared with him the Scriptures about revenge and turning the other cheek. But the young Muinane man was struggling within. He felt the new inclination toward God, but there remained the old inclination toward revenge. It is distressing for any of us to be asked to give up our hurts and our rights. The young man found it too difficult to follow Christ in forgiveness.

It was not enough for the Muinanes to simply have some right ideas about God. There had to be more than a combining of their old beliefs with those of Christianity. The Muinanes had to be reborn so they could be reshaped into the image of God.

Hymns became an important means of communicating this message to the Muinanes. One day I began to sing a hymn and an older woman grabbed her stomach, stammered something, and everyone began to laugh. She said that she was astonished that I could sing her words. That day we got the word for "astonished," which we had not been able to get before.

The first time I sang a hymn in Muinane to María Rosa, she exclaimed, "That's the prettiest thing I have ever heard." It wasn't my voice, but the words that touched her heart. From then on, nearly every time María Rosa visited, she would ask to hear the song that said, "When devils are many, look at Jesus; and when your death is near, call to Jesus." There was a time when all that the Muinanes knew was fear. They feared the thunder, lightning, devils, curses, darkness, even the rainbow. Now they had someone to talk to, someone who was greater than the devil, and larger than their fears. They could "Tell It to Jesus."

Because the Muinanes' old beliefs contrasted so sharply with Christianity, it was easy to notice when they were growing. My progress (or lack thereof) may not be so easily noticed by others, but I need to ask myself if I'm still growing. Do I know more of my Lord today than I knew yesterday?

God did not take us from electric refrigerators and gas stoves just so the Muinanes could teach us how to cook on a mud stove, hunt wild pigs, or swing a machete. We were called to fulfill our part of the Great Commission to go, to teach, and to disciple. Every believer is called to follow Christ in this way. Each of us is appointed to be God's ambassador, and designated to become a disciple-maker. It is an awesome privilege and a great responsibility.

During our years in La Sabana, the truth we spoke dispelled many myths—superstitions and omens, inaccurate worldviews, and empty religious practices. We tried to speak the truth whenever asked, but we always spoke the truth in love. In the process, we probably learned more than we taught.

Although it seems a small thing, perhaps this is one of the greatest lessons we learned in the jungle—speaking the truth in love. Speaking to God in love, speaking to others in love, and always with the voice of truth and honesty. Yes, it does seem small. But it can change the world—one heart, one soul, one mind at a time. It already has in La Sabana. It can in your world, too.

CHAPTER THIRTEEN

The River That God Remembers

Thou that hast given so much to me,
Give one thing more, a grateful heart . . .
Not thankful when it pleaseth me,
As if thy blessings had spare days,
But such a heart whose pulse may be Thy praise.
—George Herbert

JIM AND JAN'S STORY

In Jan's journal, the days of November 25 to 30, 1981, are marked: *Private, for family only!* We are both basically private people, and our inner thoughts and feelings are not easy to share with the world. But you have patiently walked with us this far; we must allow you to complete the journey.

The year 1980 found us in the final phases of translating the Muinane New Testament. Integrity in translation was crucial to us, and we agonized over every word, comma, period, and quotation mark. When the New Testament manuscripts were ready, we would take them to Wycliffe's International Linguistic Center in Dallas, Texas, where we would prepare them for the publisher.

An increase in terrorist activities in Colombia also marked the year 1980. The Dominican Republic's embassy in Bogotá was seized by terrorists. More personally traumatic to us was the discovery of a map and plan, drawn up by a terrorist group, to overrun our mission center at Lomalinda. To provide protection, the Colombian army established an outpost at Lomalinda. I was asked by the administration to be our mission's liaison with the army.

For us as a family, the new responsibility meant many days and weeks in organizing and coordinating a new aspect of our mission's program. It meant sleepless nights and times of uncertainty. But even in those busy, precarious, and unsettled days, we found the time to finish the final corrections of the Muinane New Testament manuscripts.

On January 16, 1981, Jim left Bogotá with the manuscripts, headed for Texas. Jan and Dan had gone earlier to be with Diana and her husband for the birth of our first grandson. As Jim was leaving, he chatted with a close friend, Chet Bitterman. We spoke of the mission's recent conference and our excitement that our seventeen years of translating the Muinane New Testament was almost completed.

Three days later, on January 19, seven terrorists armed with automatic weapons broke into the mission guest house in Bogotá during the early morning darkness. Not finding the branch director, the terrorists took Chet hostage, while his wife, Brenda, and their two small girls watched in terror.

Seven weeks later, Chet was murdered. Author Steve Estes writes, "They shot him just before dawn—a single bullet to the chest. Police found his body in the bus where he died, in a parking lot in the south of town. He was clean and shaven, his face relaxed. A guerrilla banner wrapped his remains" (Steve Estes, *Called to Die* [Grand Rapids: Zondervan, 1986]).

It was not wise or safe to phone Brenda until she reached the U. S. Jan talked to her shortly after she arrived in Florida, where she and her children were staying with friends.

"Brenda, is there anything at all that we can do for you?"

Brenda's answer was, "Hurry and finish the New Testament for the Muinanes."

A few months later, Brenda's brother, David Gardner, returned to visit his childhood home of Lomalinda. He brought with him the first published copies of the Muinane New Testament. Our emotions skyrocketed: we shouted with joy and wept with happiness. We could hardly wait to schedule a flight and prepare for the biggest day of our lives—the day we would bring the Bible to the Muinanes, written in their own language!

When the great day finally arrived, the first copies of the beautifully bound Muinane New Testament were packed and ready to be flown to La Sabana. We asked Clementina and her husband, Edgar, to go along to be part of the dedication service and to help with distributing the New Testaments. It all seemed so wonderful, so unbelievable, so long in coming. Seventeen years of our lives, not counting the years of schooling and preparation, had been spent to bring us to this moment. It was worth it; we were about to have the dedication of the Muinane New Testament!

It had been a year since we left the village with the manuscripts, promising to return with the published New Testament. We wished that we could inform everyone — in La Sabana, and those along the Caquetá River — of the exact day we would arrive; but that was still impossible. This area was still isolated, with no form of communication. The only way the Muinanes would know we were coming was the sound of the airplane over the treetops. They knew we would be bringing the New Testament — they would all be there.

But they weren't.

A few came to the airstrip, all those who had stayed in the village. There were not many people, however: La Sabana seemed abandoned. Those who were present were happy to see us, but they seemed quiet and uneasy. They must have sensed our disappointment. We had made the long flight to find so few people, so few to share in the excitement of the finished New Testament. But each person wanted his or her own copy of the beautiful blue book.

Arturo and his wife Albertina came by some hours later. Albertina insisted, "No, if we only have one Bible, Arturo will grab it and read it all the time. I need one of my own!"

Others arrived one by one. Some thumbed through the pages or just held it carefully, as if to say, *This book belongs*

to us; it is written in our language. The children wanted to
see the pictures. Some sat or leaned on the porch rail and
read in silence for a long time.

By the end of our short stay, every household in La
Sabana had at least one copy of the Muinane New Testament. But there was no dedication and only restrained
enthusiasm. It seemed that a silent cloud of impending
evil hung over the village. Everyone sensed it, but no one
dared speak of it. We left confused and disappointed.

The Caquetá River was rough as we headed downstream. We hoped we were heading to more peaceful,
more pleasant experiences of distributing the Muinane
New Testament.

Shortly after noon we arrived at the village of Villa
Azul, where Clementina's family now lived: Chief
Fernando, Alicia, and Clementina's brothers and sisters.
Andrés and a few others were also building houses there.
Andrés was away, however, so we did not see the one
person who had labored in translation with us from the
beginning. We saw only the support poles and frame-
work of his half-built house.

For the most part, our time at Villa Azul was good.
Everyone wanted a copy of the New Testament. Edgar
led a couple of Bible studies, and we treated a few sick
people during the days we were there. We left a box of
ten New Testaments for Andrés, which he could distrib-
ute to any who might not have received a copy. Not every
person had a New Testament, but every Muinane household had at least one.

It was a successful distribution trip, but we had
expected more. We wanted more. Aren't the people sup-

posed to be tremendously excited when the translation is finished? Isn't there always a celebration, with lots of photos of people crowding to get a copy? The Muinanes do not naturally show a lot of outward emotion except in prescribed situations, but this was even more restrained than usual.

What would we write home? We had no glowing reports of a dedication. The Muinanes were not pressing to get their first copy of the Bible. We were disappointed. We wondered if the churches back home and our other supporters would be disappointed as well. Had we failed those who had sent us? This was not the way we had planned it for seventeen years. This wasn't like the stories we had read. It was life, and it hurt!

We consoled ourselves, however, knowing that this was not the end. The Muinanes in La Sabana had suggested that we return in November when the schoolchildren would be home for break. All the men would be back, and there would be "many people for the celebration of the New Testament." We returned to Lomalinda and began preparing for November and the New Testament dedication.

We read again the accounts of other dedications and the celebrations that take place when the New Testament finally arrives. It appeared that there had never been any failures or disappointments — at least none were written about.

We approached this time in different ways. Jim tried desperately to keep his heartache as far out of mind as possible. He was certain that the God who brought us through seventeen years — sometimes harsh, punishing years—would not let us down now. Jan, who is often more cautious in her expectations, seemed to sense that reality is not only the wonderful, glamorous tales that we read and love. Sometimes life is cruel, unfair, unjust, unbearable. She acknowledged the heaviness in her heart and prepared for even more of it.

Late in November 1981, we left Lomalinda and headed toward La Sabana. Somewhere in transit, we got slightly off our heading and, although we expected to fly right over our little jungle airstrip, we bisected the river below La Sabana. Beneath us we saw a new airstrip under construction. We looked at each other sadly. There was only one possible reason for this new airstrip so close to La Sabana: drugs.

As soon as we landed in La Sabana, we felt the same sickening feeling that we had experienced in June. At that time, there were only a few to greet us. This time, no one emerged from the jungle to welcome us "home."

Some very unpleasant thoughts began to flash through our minds. We had spent nearly four hundred dollars on food and the flight to get out there. Why had the Muinanes told us that if we came in November there would be a big celebration of the New Testament, and that Muinanes from everywhere would be here? Should we stay or go back to Lomalinda? *Lord, what is going on?*

We decided to return to Lomalinda and save the cost of another flight, a few days later, to pick us up. But first, Jim went to the village to see if anyone was there. Jan had just started down the path to our house when Magdalena, Clementina's grandmother, came running to meet her. They hugged, but then Jan told her that because there were no people in La Sabana, we were planning to return on the plane to Lomalinda.

Magdalena said, "My child, what am I? I'm a person, and I am here. Don't go yet; please stay!"

We decided to stay, even if it was just to be with Magdalena. Then we found Lorenzo and some of his family. Alejandro, Regina, and their unmarried daughter were also there. We visited with them for a while. Then they returned to their houses, and we began unpacking and setting up our jungle home.

Suddenly, an airplane zoomed directly over our house. We knew by the sound that it was not a missionary plane. A few minutes later we watched two men unload some bags and boxes, which turned out to be food for the Muinanes who were working at the new airstrip downriver. About ten minutes later two men approached our house. It didn't take long for us to know for sure that they were Colombian drug dealers.

The pilot, very self-confident, came bounding up our porch steps, while the other man stayed on the ground at the foot of the steps. The second man was rough and severe. His eyes seemed to peer into every shadow and constantly darted around. He never talked, never came up the steps, never looked into our eyes; he just watched and waited.

Jan's journal best describes the thoughts and feelings that rushed through her in those moments:

I was praying as I stood in the kitchen behind the half door. *I don't understand this, Lord. Why this ending to eighteen years of loving this tribe, bringing your Word to them? Now, rejection of that love! It is hard to believe they would choose this path of great sorrow, which will only bring about the destruction of the tribe and their culture. This will likely end in death for many or all of the Muinanes. Yet, I know that among them are your chosen ones — blinded for a time, but nevertheless your children. Please give us peace in these moments right now.*

Jim went right out to greet them and invited them to sit down; the pilot did, but the bodyguard stayed at the foot of the steps. Jim's conversation with them was formal and a bit nervous. Surprisingly, the pilot and bodyguard also seemed nervous.

"We weren't expecting anyone except the Indians when we landed," the pilot said.

Jim replied, "We weren't expecting you, either."

"I'm in the fishing business," the pilot lied smoothly. "While the Indians are fishing for me they need good food."

We found out later that he had brought rice, flour, canned sardines, a lot of processed food, and cases of Coca-Cola. He also brought radio/cassette players as big as suitcases, as well as a small gas generator. The people told us he used the generator for light, so the cocaine can be processed at night. He told Jim that he brought it for the mothers who needed light in order to nurse their babies at night.

The pilot told us several stories and then the conversation turned to the subject of the guerrillas, or terrorists. He said he couldn't fly at all in the Caquetá now because of the guerrillas. "There's just no peace anywhere," he complained.

"No," Jim responded, "if you don't have peace in your own heart, if you don't have peace with God, there is no peace in this world." Jim showed him a copy of the New Testament and explained, "This is why we came here eighteen years ago, to bring the peace of God to these people." The cocaine dealer hurriedly flipped through the New Testament politely, then handed it back, saying, "Well, I guess I've ruined your work for you."

Before Jim could respond, the crackle of our two-way radio caught the drug dealer's attention.

We normally left the radio on to monitor the progress of our plane as it returned to Lomalinda. We always felt better when we knew that the plane had safely returned over that vast, unforgiving stretch of jungle and had set down on the airstrip at Lomalinda.

"Is that a radio?" the drug dealer demanded nervously.

We immediately sensed danger, for at that point, we became a threat. Would they fear exposure? What might fear cause them to do? "Yes, thanks for reminding me," Jim answered. "I guess it is about time for me to shut it down for the day. Our plane should have landed safely at Lomalinda by now. Would you care to come in and listen while I sign off the air?" The radio operator would not expect us to advise them when we shut the radio off, but today was different. Would they understand? More important, would the operator betray any surprise or concern?

The drug dealer stepped through the door, into our house, and followed Jim to the shelf where the radio sat crackling. Jim pushed in the button on the microphone and spoke in Spanish, "Lomalinda, Lomalinda, La Sabana calling Lomalinda. Do you copy me?"

High-school student Kim Grant was in the radio tower that afternoon. Without hesitation, without asking why we were calling in, without a hint of surprise that the call was in Spanish, Kim's voice came back, also in Spanish, "Sabana, Sabana, we copy you loud and clear."

Jim told Kim that we had a visiting aircraft for the night and that we were turning the radio off; but he would check in early the next day in case they would need us to stand by. *Click,* and we were off the air.

The drug dealer understood every word we spoke in Spanish, and we hoped that his fears would be calmed. If we had spoken in English, he might have worried that we were turning him in.

Somehow we knew, by the way Kim answered our strange call in Spanish, that she sensed the danger we were in and would alert others at Lomalinda to pray. Hundreds of miles of jungle, and twelve hours of darkness, lay between us and the nearest person who spoke English. The only one who could protect us in the middle of the Amazon jungle was the One we contacted by prayer. Somehow we felt better. The drug dealer, satisfied we had not reported him to the authorities, left with his bodyguard to spend the night at one of the Indian's houses.

We didn't sleep much that night. We had not fully learned the lessons of King David, who said, "I will both lay me down in peace, and sleep: for thou, Lord, only makest me dwell in safety" (Ps. 4:8). Still, despite our fears and worries, we did eventually drift off to sleep.

We were awakened at 5:30 the next morning by the noise of the drug plane taking off in the thickest fog imaginable. Flying in the fog is dangerous, but they had to get the processed drug to a drop-off point, where they are paid, before the flight was detected by the military or by Colombia's civil air authorities. In recent months there had been reports of six planes going down in the jungle because of these early morning flights. Sometimes the early ground fog does not break, and they get lost and run out of gas.

That afternoon Pablo arrived. He had paddled a day and a half upriver to catch us before we left. He didn't talk a lot, and we didn't ask many questions. We didn't have to. He paid for his nephew's flight passage, from a year before, with a thousand-peso bill. He did tell us that he had read Matthew through Luke and hadn't found a mistake. He also said, "Don't come back until after April. Maybe we will be free then. I'm worried that something terrible will happen to you, or to us, if you come back sooner."

When old Alejandro came to visit, he said, "They have come to get the *jübiho* (cocaine)."

Jim said, "It looks just like the days of your fathers, when the rubber barons killed almost all of the Muinanes . . . and now it is starting all over again."

Alejandro never answered. His eyes filled with tears as he descended the steps of our house and slowly walked away.

Alejandro, like Granny, was a teenager when almost all of the Muinanes were killed by outsiders. Again, in his lifetime, he was seeing history repeat itself. Alejandro, his wife Regina, and Magdalena know the end. They live in fear of what lies ahead, as the Muinanes walk again this path of history. During our visit, they all seemed plagued by memories too awful to recall, feelings too deep and painful to discuss—the terrible realization that it was starting all over again.

For weeks and months afterwards, we cried. It wasn't supposed to end this way. We were filled with conflicting emotions—anger, sorrow, fear. Like Alejandro, we wanted to walk away and pretend it wasn't real. But we couldn't wave away eighteen years of our life and say only, "Oh well, it didn't work out."

We had always thought that with God's help we could change anything, make everything right, correct every mistake, make everything fair. But life is not equal, or fair, or always just. We live in an imperfect world, made that way by sin. "We know that the whole creation has been groaning as in the pains of childbirth right up to the present time. Not only so, but we ourselves, who have the firstfruits of the Spirit, groan inwardly as we wait eagerly for our adoption as sons, the redemption of our bodies" (Rom. 8:22-23,NIV). We may see a dramatic change in the people we minister to; or we may be called only to plant, water, and toil, never seeing the end of our work. We can be sure, however, that all will be ended in the way that God intends it to be.

Everything will find its fullness in Christ, who weaves together sowing and reaping, good days and bad, heartache and victory, into a tapestry of praise to himself. We know that there are no "spare" days when it comes to God's mercy and grace. Each day always has enough grace in it to supply our every need.

We are convinced that this is not the end. The final chapter of the Muinane story will not be written by rubber barons or cocaine lords. The curtain of history did not drop because we were disappointed. Final accounts are not settled until the day when God allows eternity to swallow up time. It is God who must establish the work of our hands (Ps. 90:17).

Often in life, we want to see the end now. We want the pain to stop instantly, the stress to pass, the agony of defeat to be removed and replaced by the joy of victory. Sometimes the pressure is so great that we lose the desire to play the game. It's during these times, when we don't understand, that we must trust God and go on. The Cross was not the end: the Resurrection lies ahead. No matter how bad, how bleak, how desperate things are right now, now is not the end.

Someday God will settle all accounts and right the wrongs. Some accounts may be settled early, and a few people may see the victories and enjoy the rewards on this earth. These are the stories we write, the experiences we enjoy recalling, the people we applaud. But for most of us, life is a continuing journey of reality. There are joys and victories along the way, along with the hurts and disappointments. Victory is not permanent in this life, and failure is never final.

Someday the world will dissolve and break apart with a great noise, as the final flaming curtain of fire brings an end to time (2 Pet. 3:10-12). Then every injustice will be corrected, every tear dried, every hurt healed, every heartache removed. In eternity we will stand next to Muinanes, who will also be in that "great multitude, which no man could number, of all nations, and kindreds, and people, and tongues" (Rev. 7:9).

And when you stand before God, remember the Muinanes you have met here—those who, having placed their faith in Christ, will be standing next to you:

Alejandro	Margarita ("Granny")
Andrés	Magdalena
Arturo	Manuel
Clementina	Cecilia
Chief Fernando	Regina
Alicia	Virgelina

At that time you will meet other Muinanes:

Adelina	Oliverio
Albertina	Otillia
Alberto	Pablo
Aniceto	Rosa
Cleotilde	Selmira
Inez	Sebastían
Jaime	Sophía
Misael	

. . . and all those who put their trust in the "living God, who is the Savior of all" (1 Tim. 4:10). There will be no disappointment then!

So until that day:

Stay on the path,
keep the Chief in sight,

continue to follow, even when your knees ache, or your heart breaks.

You need never fear that God will forget. God remembers your name and the plans he has for your life. He knows the paths you will walk, the hills you will climb, the bridges you must cross, the rivers you will navigate. And on those paths, you will see the footprints of God — the evidence that he has gone before you and still walks beside you, every step of the way.

We found the footprints of God on those jungle trails. He was there before us, and he will be there long after we are gone from this earth. The "forgotten river" flows not only into the Amazon, but also beyond that, to the throne of God. And back from the throne, and from the Lamb, flows the "river of the water of life" (Rev. 22:1, NIV).

There is no such place as "the river that God forgot." Every river — every soul — is the one that God remembers.

Other Books and Articles by the Authors

James W. Walton, "Muinane Diagnostic Use of Narcotics." In *Economic Botany* vol. 24 no. 2 (New York: New York Botanical Gardens, 1970).

James W. and Janice P. Walton, "Phonemes of Muinane." In *Phonemic Systems of Colombian Languages.* ed. by Benjamin F. Elson (Norman, Oklahoma: SIL, 1967).

— — —, "Muinane." In *Aspectos de la Cultura Material de Grupos Etnicos de Colombia* (Colombia: Ministerio de Gobierno, 1973), 137–160.

— — —, *Una Gramatica de la Lengua Muinane.* (Colombia: Ministerio de Gobierno/Instituto Lingüístico de Verano, 1975).

— — —, "Participant Reference and Introducers in Muinane Clause and Paragraph." In *Discourse Grammar: Studies in Indian Languages of Colombia, Panama and Ecuador,* ed. by Robert E. Longacre and Frances Woods, Part 3 (Dallas, Texas: SIL, 1976). 45–65.

— — —, "Muinane." In *Estudios en Andoke y Muinane* (Lomalinda, Colombia: Ministerio de Gobierno/ILV, 1981), 37–47.

181